THE DEVIL'S MISTRESS

The Devil's Mistress was going to be an important film, and Natasha was thrilled to be playing the lead—until she discovered that her leading man was going to be none other than Alex Brent, with whom she had had such a passionate and disastrous relationship several years ago. And who, she soon realised, still hated and distrusted her as much as he ever had . . .

THE DEVIL'S MISTRESS

BY

SARAH HOLLAND

MILLS & BOON LIMITED
15–16 BROOK'S MEWS
LONDON W1A 1DR

First published 1982
Australian copyright 1982
Philippine copyright 1982
This edition 1982

© Sarah Holland 1982

ISBN 0 263 74001 3

Set in Monophoto Times 11 on 11½ pt.
01–1182 – 46817

Made and printed in Great Britain by
Richard Clay (The Chaucer Press) Ltd,
Bungay, Suffolk

For
Jeanie Devine

CHAPTER ONE

NATASHA slid out of bed with a yawn and ruffled her long golden hair. Yesterday's travelling had tired her out, but after a good night's sleep she had a more than healthy appetite. The hum of traffic passing by the hotel made her look towards the huge gilt-edged French windows of her balcony. Nice was coming alive.

It's going to be a beautiful day, she thought with a smile. She wandered into the bathroom and brushed her teeth before taking a quick shower. Perhaps she would spend the day on the beach, relaxing in the hot sleepy atmosphere. Or she could always explore Nice.

She smiled at the thought of a lazy holiday. Until they found Lynx, there would be little or no work to do. They had been searching for the perfect man to play Lynx for a year—without success.

There was a knock on the door and Natasha stepped out of the shower. That, she thought hungrily, will be breakfast.

'*Moment, s'il vous plaît!*' she called, reaching for the ivory lace negligee and belting it at her slender waist. A moment later the door opened, and a young, dark-haired waiter came in with her breakfast.

'*Bonjour*, Mademoiselle Fox,' he breathed, gazing at her in open admiration.

Natasha smiled sadly as he left, knowing he only saw Natasha Fox—actress; the petite, slender-boned lady with a shimmering curtain of golden hair which framed a face of delicate beauty, fine bones surrounding a pair of huge cornflower blue eyes which held a breathtaking vulnerability.

The publicity machine adored Natasha; but she despised it. The press latched on to the air of innocence and vulnerability which she had—not realising that she *was* vulnerable, easily hurt. 'You're too sensitive!' Marney had often told her.

Marney was her agent and close friend. He hid behind an image of Santa Claus with his round, always jolly face—but he was shrewd, street-wise, and he didn't fool Natasha.

'You bring out the father in men,' Marney would tell her, approving of her taste in clothes. She loved to wear Victorian lace, mainly white, long flowing sleeves and wide-brimmed white hats. Once she had bought a white lace parasol and the press had gone crazy, calling her the Edwardian Princess. 'They take one look at your baby-blue eyes and want to protect you from the world,' Marney kept saying.

Natasha sat down to breakfast, pouring steaming coffee into her cup and dipping a flaky croissant into it, biting into the pastry with relish. Then she flicked open the British newspaper on her lap.

Her face drained of all colour as she stared at the face on the page. Cruel black eyes looked back at her, mocking her as she read the caption next to the picture. It couldn't be true! It was a trick, a joke. Someone had pulled a publicity stunt.

She jerked the paper shut with white-knuckled

hands, staring into space for a dazed moment. No one would agree to it. No one who really knew her would let it happen.

She opened the paper again. Alex Brent's dark, brooding face watched her, his eyes stabbing at her, the cruel firm mouth twisted with sardonic amusement.

She read the caption: '... Alex Brent, internationally famous actor of stage and screen, playboy, jet-setter, hero of millions, has been chosen to star as Lynx, in the forthcoming production of *The Devil's Mistress*.'

'No!' she whispered in shocked disbelief. They must have got it wrong. Her frown was etched with pain, her small white teeth biting into her lip.

She had to find out if it was true. But who could she ring? Surely if Marney had known, he would have warned her long ago? She slowly reached for the telephone and dialled a number.

'Marney?' she said softly, one eye on the newspaper as the receiver at the other end was picked up.

'Natasha! How are you feeling, sweetheart?'

She detected a sound of worry in his voice. He was playing it cool. 'Marney,' she said in a shaky voice, 'what's going on?'

There was a little silence at the other end, then Marney sighed. 'Listen, angel, I couldn't do anything about it. By the time I knew who they wanted you to co-star with, it was too late to back out on the contract. They could have sued us for millions, honey—millions! When I think of it, it makes me want to ...'

But Natasha wasn't listening, she was staring in horror at the wall, her eyes wide, her mouth trembling. She couldn't do it, not in a million years. Spend months filming with Alex? After all this time? After all that had happened between them? She shivered, her hands shaking with sudden shock.

'Honey? Natasha, are you listening to me?' Marney sounded very worried as he called her back to reality.

'Yes,' she said shakily. 'Yes, I'm listening.' Her eyes flicked back to the photograph of Alex, the winged sardonic brows, thick black hair and almost Satanic eyes which had held no pity for her while she cried.

'I was gonna break it gently to you, angel, you've got to believe me,' said Marney, then swore under his breath, 'But those goddamned hounds got news of it sooner than I expected.'

Marney hated the press when they didn't do exactly what he wanted them to. Normally they were his best friends.

Natasha took a deep breath. 'I don't want to do it, Marney. I can't!' And that's understating the case, she thought with a sad smile. 'Is there any way we can get out of it?' She held her breath hopefully.

'Sorry, sweetheart, really I am,' Marney said with a sigh. 'But if we wriggle on that contract, they'll have our guts for garters—and that's putting it mildly! All that publicity about Sabrina and Lynx, all that hoo-hah about who was going to play Lynx—we just couldn't swing it.' He sighed again. 'There's just no way.'

Natasha bit deep into her lip. She was trapped. There was no way out. *The Devil's Mistress* had caught the public's attention, and spread a fever like wildfire. The part she was playing was practically made for her—she had been picked immediately as the hauntingly beautiful heroine, Sabrina.

Sabrina; the silver-haired heroine who was like a sea-nymph, a mermaid. Her counterpart was strong; Lynx—the black-haired man who controlled her, made her love him, took her submission with cruel black eyes until their passion for each other consumed them in the flames of eternity.

Alex Brent was perfect for the part. He *was* Lynx.

'Natasha, I've got more bad news for you,' Marney was telling her in a careful voice, worried about her reaction to his news.

She frowned, feeling a sense of unease. But what could be worse than the shock she had already had? 'Go ahead, Marney,' she said quietly. 'I'm numb already, I don't think you'll have much impact.'

'They want a meeting today,' Marney said flatly. 'You, me, Alex Brent and International.'

She sucked her breath in. That was too much to ask! She felt drained of all belief in herself, her confidence suddenly ripped to shreds.

She shook her head briefly. 'No,' she said, her voice breaking a little. 'Sorry, can't do it.' She bit her lip quickly, feeling tears prick her lids. What could she say to Alex? How would she react?

'Hush now,' Marney soothed in a paternal

manner, 'it won't be as bad as all that.'

'It will,' her voice was barely a whisper. 'You don't know what happened.' She felt a tear escape from beneath her lid, and run down her smooth cheek.

'Listen, angel, I'll be right behind you. You've got to go through with it sooner or later, and today is as good a day as any.' He paused, listening intently because he wasn't sure if he had heard her start to cry or not. 'Besides,' he tried to cheer her up, 'you're an actress, aren't you? One of the best!'

She couldn't smile. 'I'm not being funny, Marney,' she said in a soft barely audible voice, 'I just can't do it.' Look into those eyes again? She would feel everything all over again, be plunged into all the pain she had ever felt.

'Sure you can!' encouraged Marney. 'Listen, you go out there and give them the greatest performance of your life, give it all you've got. Honey, you'll have them dancing in the aisles!'

'Marney——' she began, but he interrupted her hurriedly.

'I'll pick you up at noon. Wear something stunning.'

The phone went dead in her hands. Natasha replaced it numbly in its cradle and stared out to sea. Marney was doing his best; it wasn't his fault International had picked Alex. Marney found other people's pain unbearable—that was why he shied away from it; it hurt him too much.

Perhaps she was scared for nothing. She glanced at Alex's face in the newspaper and saw the hardboned face mocking her. No, she wasn't scared for nothing; she had every reason to be scared. She shivered.

Alex Brent was a very dangerous man, and he could still hurt her if she let him.

The car sped towards Monaco, eating up the small distance of the Promenade des Anglais, the long, palm tree-lined sea-front, in no time at all. Then they were on the coastal road, and Natasha looked up at the rock-hewn scenery, the rough green shrubbery which grew along the towering cliffs.

Her slender hands plucked restlessly at her lace dress and she looked across at Marney with worried eyes. 'Who else will be there?' Her quiet voice belied the tremors which ran through her.

Marney patted her hand with a broad smile. 'I told you—just you, me, Alex and B.B. Jackson. It'll be fine—I know you. You could act anyone off the stage and down to Timbuctoo if you wanted to.'

She looked away. She was an actress and she was good, but not that good. She didn't see how she could disguise her feelings for Alex, because they ran too deep.

They drove down into Monte Carlo, and butterflies leapt about in her stomach. Her heart was beating much too fast as they pulled up outside the hotel.

'Chin up, angel,' Marney whispered in her ear as he led her up into the hotel and through to the restaurant lounge.

She whitened visibly as, across the room, she met a pair of cruel black eyes, watching her with a

mocking smile on hard, sensual lips. His thick
black hair was still vibrant, silky, his body still held
that lean hard whipcord strength.

'Alex,' she whispered through dry lips, and
Marney turned to study her with concern etched
into his frown.

'*Courage, mon brave,*' said Marney worriedly, 'or
something like that.' He nudged her, and led her
forward to where the men were seated with their
drinks.

B.B. Jackson jumped out of his seat. 'Natasha!'
he exclaimed, pumping her hand. 'Wonderful to
see you!' He was the producer of the film. He had
an incredible, livewire energy which had apparently
burnt every hair except three off his head, leaving
him as bald as an egg.

She smiled, not daring to look away from him,
in case she saw Alex. 'Hello, B.B. It's lovely to see
you again.' She had always liked him; he had a
genuine warmth and enthusiasm for life and
people, and was well liked and respected.

B.B. waved a fat cigar between his podgy fingers
and ran a hand through his three black hairs. 'I
want you to meet Mr Alex Brent—or should I call
you Lynx?' He roared with laughter.

Natasha felt her muscles lock together as she
turned slowly to look at Alex. What would he say
to her? How could she speak to him? After all these
years, to meet now.

Alex stood up, his long lean legs uncoiling
slowly. He towered over her, six foot four of
rugged, hard power, and said,

'Hello, Miss Fox. I'm very pleased to meet you.'

His sensual lips twisted into a smile as he took her hand.

Her heart stopped in sheer incredulity. He didn't remember her. She had almost committed suicide because he had hurt her so badly, and he didn't even remember her face!

Her eyes searched his for a spark of recognition, but there was none. 'Mr Brent,' she managed to stammer out through aching lips.

She looked down at her hand, so slender and pale, held by his strong tanned hand—it was such a contrast, and so indicative of their relationship. He could crush her without an effort.

Lunch was agonising. The food tasted like sawdust, and her appetite seemed to have been washed away by pain. Her eyes met Alex's many times across the table, and she flinched every time the memories came back.

'We've got a big hit on our hands,' B.B. was saying, waving his cigar about with a flourish. 'I can feel it in my guts—and when I feel it in my guts, I rely on it.' He patted his stomach. 'I've got very reliable guts!' He roared with laughter.

Alex was watching Natasha across the table, his black eyes narrowed with amusement. 'And of course,' he said in a voice like black velvet, 'Miss Fox is the perfect Sabrina.'

Natasha looked up, her eyes meeting his with a jolt. 'Thank you,' she murmured, her hands pleating the tablecloth restlessly.

Alex watched her, a smile playing with his lips. 'So delicate,' he murmured smokily. 'Almost like

porcelain . . . why, I could crush you——' he closed
his tanned fist slowly, 'like that.'

She looked at him, startled. It was almost as
though he could read her mind. A shiver ran down
her spine and she stared, mesmerised as though he
was a sleek jungle cat, prowling around her.

Marney was watching, worried. 'Why don't you
call her Natasha?' he asked Alex, looking at him
with carefully concealed dislike. 'It makes her feel
a lot easier.'

Alex flicked his black lashes, his gaze switching
to Marney. 'I don't recall addressing you,' he said
succinctly.

B.B. watched, amazed, then he jumped into
action. 'Good old Alex,' he said with an attempt at
joviality, his eyes darting around the three faces at
the table. 'He's getting ready to play Lynx—
dangerous man, Lynx!'

He doesn't have to act, thought Natasha, shivering, he's already dangerous. She still felt numb
inside after realising that he didn't remember her.
She was just another girl to him, another face,
another body, another voice. She felt a surge of
bitterness, damped down by a stab of pain as she
bit her lip and fought hard to keep control.

Coffee arrived and she was relieved. She wanted
to get out of there, run back to the safety of her
hotel.

Alex watched her through a haze of silver blue
cigar smoke, his lids half closed. 'I understand we
start filming next month.'

B.B. answered him with a wide smile. 'That's
right, Alex. So I hope you and the little lady will

take time out to get to know each other.' He winked at Alex. 'But not too well—I don't want you to lose any chemistry!'

Alex looked back at Natasha. 'In that case,' he murmured, 'I think it might be a good idea if I escorted her back to her hotel.'

There was a little silence, then Natasha said hurriedly, 'No, please don't,' she looked at Marney in desperation, 'That isn't necessary. Marney can take me back.'

Alex turned that cutting gaze on to Marney, and smiled, showing sharp white teeth. 'You don't mind, do you, Marney?' he asked, his face daring him to disagree.

'Well, I . . . er . . .' Marney spluttered, scratching his head and looking at B.B. for guidance.

Natasha bit her lip. How could she possibly stop him? He always got his own way in the end—he was ruthless. But she couldn't bear the thought of sitting in a car with him and pretending they were strangers. He had ripped her life apart.

'Nonsense!' B.B. waved any protests aside and smiled broadly at Natasha. 'I think it's an excellent idea. Might spice the action up a little if you knew the exact characters each played.'

That was the last thing Natasha wanted. She gave Marney one last pleading look, but he just shrugged. There was nothing he could do about it if B.B. approved.

Alex stood up. He looked sensational in a white close-fitting blazer, a sexy blue and white striped shirt and beautifully cut dark blue trousers, a razor-sharp crease emphasising the length of his muscular legs.

'Gentlemen,' he said, giving them a brief smile before coming round to Natasha and helping her out of her chair.

She said, 'goodbye,' to Marney and B.B., her heart beating fast, her pulses skipping in her ears. Her legs felt like water as she stood up, but she was trapped, and she knew it.

Alex took her arm, but she refused to look at him. They walked slowly out to the foyer of the hotel, and Natasha felt her hands start shaking as they went out to the heat of the July sunshine which beat down on Monte Carlo.

Alex opened the car door for her and helped her in before walking with lazy grace round to his side of the car. 'Which hotel are you in?' he asked as he slid the ignition keys in and started the engine.

Natasha stared straight ahead. 'The Negresco,' she said in a soft, shaky voice. She didn't dare look at him, in case he saw through her eyes into her heart. She could act all she liked with her voice and her face—but her eyes were a mirror of her soul.

They drove in silence to Nice, and Natasha's nerves were in shreds by the time they arrived. Her hands were clammy, her eyes restless, darting. Her muscles ached with the pretence of not knowing him, not loving him.

Alex switched the engine off. 'Shall we go in?' he murmured, his eyes flicking over her face.

She swallowed, shaking her head quickly. 'No . . . thank you. I'm rather tired.' She just wanted to get away from him.

Alex watched her for a moment, then got out of the car and walked lazily round to her side, helping her on to the pavement. 'I'm sure you'll feel better after a cool drink,' he said.

'No, really . . .' Natasha began as he took her arm with one strong hand and led her into the hotel.

The marble floor echoed with their footsteps, the glass chandeliers overhead jangling in the slight breeze. Natasha bit her lip, looking up at him sideways. He still frightened her as much as he ever had.

'I'll see you to your room,' he said in a dark voice after she had collected her key.

'No, really,' she said breathlessly, her hands twisting the key as she looked at him, 'there's no need.'

But Alex merely looked at her and took her arm again, leading her to the lift which was hidden from view by marble pillars. He pressed the call button.

'My dear,' he drawled against her ear as the lift arrived, 'I can remember when you used to beg me to come to your room.'

She whitened, looking at him, seeing the cruel mocking black eyes laughing at her, his sensual mouth twisted into a smile. He reminded her of Satan himself.

'Get away from me!' she whispered, flushing with hot colour as she tried to turn and run.

He gripped her arms with hands like steel and pulled her into the lift to land hard against him. Her heart was beating hard against his chest, her breathing unsteady.

The winged brows rose with amusement. 'Did you think I'd forgotten you, Natasha?'

She stared at him with hatred and fear. 'Yes,' she whispered, her hands shaking as she tried to struggle away from him.

Alex gave a harsh, mocking laugh. 'Forget you?' he asked, and his eyes ran insolently over her body, resting on her high, firm breasts which rose and fell with her laboured breathing. 'How could I forget you?' He looked back at her face. 'Your body came to life under my hands.'

She flushed hotly, her eyes stinging with unshed tears. He had brought her body to life, only to kill it when he was finished with her. 'Don't remind me,' she muttered, 'I don't want to remember.'

'Ah, but you do,' he murmured, his hands leaving her arms to travel down sensuously over her body, the long fingers splaying over her breasts. 'You see?' He drawled as her heart thudded rapidly and her face flushed with heat at his touch, 'You enjoy my touch.'

Natasha shivered with fear. 'Get your hands off me,' she said breathlessly, trying to push him away, 'Don't touch me!' What was he doing to her? I should hate him she thought, I should feel angry when he touches me. But he was flooding her with heated excitement.

The lift doors slid open, and Natasha nearly fell out. Her legs were weak as she tried to run down the corridor to the safety of her room, but Alex was too fast.

His hand gripped her wrist as she reached the

door of her room. 'Not so fast, my love,' he drawled, his fingers biting into her. 'I might get the impression you're trying to run away from me.'

Natasha shrank away from him, wide-eyed. 'You're hurting me,' she said shakily, her blue eyes vivid in her pale face. She felt so small beside his obvious strength.

He raised one dark brow. 'Am I?' he looked down at her fragile, captive wrist, then leaned over and slowly took the keys from her before releasing her.

Natasha watched him as he unlocked the door and opened it, leading her in and closing it behind them. He put the keys on the side table in the entrance to her room.

'We'll have a drink to celebrate our reunion, shall we?' he said. He watched her as she slowly went into the room and stood in the centre.

Alex walked over to the mini-fridge and took out a small bottle of champagne. He eyed her with mocking amusement. 'The best vintage, I think,' he said, uncorking it and pouring it into two crystal champagne glasses, 'because only the best will do for an occasion like this.'

I can't bear it, she thought. He was mocking her, attacking her with his clever tongue and ruthless wit. I'd prefer to think he's forgotten me.

'Please, stop this,' she said quietly, her hands twisting together as she looked down at the floor in painful humiliation. 'I don't understand why you're doing it.'

Alex handed her a glass of champagne with a smile, his cruel eyes on hers. 'The toast is us, my sweet,' he drawled, standing very close to her. 'Drink.' His sinewy hand moved to tilt the glass to her lips and Natasha swallowed, choking on the bubbles. Alex laughed. 'You never could take your drink.'

She flushed. She knew very well what he was referring to. 'I choked on the bubbles,' she said by way of explanation.

He laughed again, watching her. 'Ah, but there are no bubbles in wine,' he pointed out, moving closer to her, 'are there?'

She bent her head, crimsoning. 'No,' she whispered.

Alex moved one hand to the back of her head, running his fingers through the long golden curtain of her hair. 'And after sharing two bottles of wine with someone, you might just lose your head altogether.' His hands began to tighten on her hair.

She looked up, her eyes wide and filled with pain. 'Please stop it, Alex,' she begged. He was hurting her with his words, bringing back all the pain of her teenage love affair.

Alex grasped a handful of her hair at the back of her head, bringing her head up, her face turned to his. 'Remind me how much you can lose your head, Natasha,' he said thickly, his black eyes focusing on her pale, full mouth. 'Show me again.'

His hot mouth clamped down on hers, bringing a sweet rush of excitement. Natasha clung to him, her legs weak, her heart hammering inside her. Their bodies pressed together with a renewal of passion, his hands sliding up and down her sensually. She moaned from somewhere deep in the back of her throat.

The champagne glass slipped from her fingers, thudding on the deep carpet, a stain seeping into the soft pink colour. Her hands curled in his hair, stroking him.

Alex raised his head, his eyes glittering, his face flushed beneath his tan. 'You're still the most exciting creature I've ever made love to, Natasha,' he murmured, his breathing unsteady, his heart thudding against his chest.

She caught her breath. How could she have made such a fool of herself? It had been crazy, to allow herself to respond that way, but she couldn't help herself. Her body turned to liquid fire the moment he touched her with those strong brown hands.

Her eyes flashed with pain. 'You're wrong if you think I enjoyed it,' she lied, trying to pull away from him. 'I hated it!'

Alex gave a harsh crack of laughter. 'Do you think I'm a fool? I felt the way you kissed me back.'

She flushed, bending her head quickly so he couldn't see the tell-tale colour of her cheeks. 'You are a fool, Alex,' she said in a steady voice. 'You're bigger and stronger than me, and if I didn't give in to you you would beat me into submission.'

There was a little silence. Then Alex said in a deep voice, 'I've never hit a woman in my life and you know it.'

She looked up at him, feeling her lie was working. 'Not yet, but I wouldn't put it past you. You use force to get what you want, and I'd rather kiss you back than be forced into it.'

A tide of deep red flooded his face and he swore under his breath. 'You're lying!' he said angrily.

She *was* lying, but she couldn't back down now. 'I kissed you because you frighten me,' she replied, her eyes searching his to see into his mind. But it was useless—they were like polished jet.

His mouth hardened into a firm straight line and his hands tightened on her shoulders, the fingers biting into her flesh. 'At least I arouse some emotion in you,' he said between his teeth. 'I wouldn't want to leave you indifferent.'

Natasha shivered. She started to try and ease herself out of his grasp, twisting away from him.

'Running away, Natasha?' he asked as he twisted her hands behind her back, pinioning her. 'You always seem to be running away. You spend your whole life running.'

She looked at him angrily, her blue eyes flashing. 'Oh no, Alex, I didn't do the running.' Her mouth tightened as the memory returned. 'I was the poor fool who got left behind.'

There was a tense silence. Then Alex's mouth twisted, his cruel eyes mocking her. 'Perhaps that will teach you not to invite too many men to your bed.'

She sucked her breath in. The insult left her speechless for a few tense seconds. Then she said, 'You always were a cruel bastard,' in a breathless voice. 'But this time I don't want anything to do with you.' She twisted harder, pulling away from him as hard as she could.

They struggled together. 'Stop fighting me, damn you!' Alex bit out.

She pushed him away with a supreme effort and ran full pelt to the door, yanking it open while he was still off balance, and ran down the corridor to the stairs before he could follow. She ran as fast as she could, knowing Alex would assume she had taken the lift.

She was out of the hotel before he caught up with her, but she heard him calling her name, coming after her. Her heart pounded with fear as she ran round the corner by the hotel and into a shopping street. Her eyes darted frantically for a hiding place.

Alex's footsteps were ringing out behind her as he followed. She took a deep breath and dived into a shop, hiding behind a bookstand and waiting with trembling hands in case he had seen her.

She held her breath, waiting for several minutes, but he didn't come in. She exhaled with relief, then realised that the people in the shop were watching her curiously.

'Mademoiselle?' enquired the puzzled shop-keeper, and Natasha busily hunted around the books, pretending great interest. She bought a French paperback for a few francs and hurriedly made her exit.

Outside in the street, there was no sign of Alex. She went back to the hotel, but his car had gone. She realised she had left her key in the room and would have to get a spare from the desk.

But she was relieved that Alex had left her in

peace. For now. She shivered, suddenly seeing his face in her mind.

She knew he would be back.

CHAPTER TWO

THE next day Natasha woke up feeling emotionally bruised. Her mind was filled with images of Alex, of his anger and his cruelty. She tried to banish him from her mind, but it was useless. He hung on, mocking her, as though aware that he was driving her out of her mind.

She went down to the beach, which was a mistake, because lying in the hot glare of the sun all day did little to help matters. All she could do was think. She lay back on the blue and white striped mattress and tried to sleep.

It was a beautiful day. Nice was sometimes prone to bouts of rain and greyness, but today the sun was out in full strength. It sizzled down on her, making her eyelids heavy, droplets of sweat running slowly from her forehead. She wasn't really supposed to tan for filming. It ruined many shots, because the tan had to be kept even. She moved under the blue-striped parasol above her, shading herself from the sun and watching the pretty white fringing wave softly in the sea breeze.

The beach was packed, and Natasha had been lucky to get a place on one of the mattress loungers. She ignored the avid glances of young men who eyed her delightedly, their gazes running over her long, curvaceous body in the bright yellow bikini.

She had lunch on the beach in the enchanting

restaurant there. The atmosphere was relaxed and warm as she sat on a wicker chair, drinking iced lemonade. She was beginning to feel rather less nervous by the time she had to leave and go back to the hotel.

She had been a little worried in case she saw Alex on the beach. But then the beach was exclusively for people staying at the Negresco, and she knew Alex wasn't staying anywhere in Nice.

I wonder where he *is* staying, she thought with a frown as she went slowly across the busy road, dodging cars as she crossed. He hadn't mentioned it yesterday, but she had an idea he would have told her if he was in the same hotel as she was.

She got back to her room at six o'clock, feeling the heat clinging on to her skin. A shower, she decided, was the best way to liven herself up. She stripped and stepped under the warm jets of water, feeling it wash away the sweat and sun lotion in one fell swoop. It cooled her head, and made her ears buzz less.

She stepped out of the shower, peering into the mirror as she wrapped a large bath towel around herself. I hope I haven't overdone it, she thought with a frown, studying her golden, flushed skin.

When she went back into her bedroom she jerked back, gasping in shock. Alex lay casually on the bed, watching her.

He raised one dark brow. 'Cat got your tongue?'

Natasha swallowed, her heart beginning to thud a little faster as she looked back at him. 'How did you get in?' she asked, her hands going immediately to tighten the bath towel at her breasts.

He watched her for a moment, then reached his hand inside his jacket pocket. 'Not very observant, are you?' he drawled, pulling out her door key. He held it up in front of her. 'In future I suggest you keep your eyes open a little and think more.'

'Give me that!' she snapped angrily, snatching at the key. It was stupid of her not to have realised he still had the key. He must have picked it up before following her yesterday.

Alex tilted his black head up, his eyes challenging her. 'Come and get it,' he dared softly.

She wanted to slap his arrogant face, but instead she controlled her temper and forced herself to act naturally. She walked over to the fridge and opened it, taking out a chilled bottle of Perrier water. 'What would be the point?' she asked, shrugging. 'I'd be fighting a losing battle.'

His eyes narrowed. 'I always play to win,' he said succinctly, 'I'd be a fool if I did otherwise.'

Natasha poured herself a glass of water, watching the bubbles spurt about in the glass, rising to the top. She watched him from the safety of her lashes, wondering how on earth she could get the key back.

Alex followed her gaze, his mind immediately tuning in with hers. 'Don't try it,' he warned lazily. 'If you made a sudden lunge towards me I might just take it as a compliment.'

She believed him. He was quite capable of wrestling with her on the bed just because she had tried to get her own key back. 'What do you want, Alex?' she asked flatly.

'What a charming question,' he drawled, his eyes

insulting as they travelled over her body. 'You do say the most naïve things!'

Her cheeks flamed as his eyes rested on the bare golden length of her thighs. 'That was all over a long time ago!' she snapped, her eyes hating him as she met his gaze. 'Say whatever it is you have to say and then get out!'

Her words and tone angered him, and he stood up, his mouth hardening as he took a step towards her. 'Don't speak to me like that again, Natasha,' he grated.

She shivered at the menace in his voice, and her hand shook as she raised the glass of water to her parched lips. The slightly acidic taste of the bubbles stung her, calming her jumping nerves.

She turned her back on him, forcing herself to speak in a controlled voice. 'There's nothing between us any more,' she said, her hands fiddling restlessly with the glasses on top of the fridge, 'I can speak to you in any way I choose to.'

He moved restlessly behind her, and Natasha moistened her lips with her tongue, listening intently to the silence that followed. Then she felt him right behind her, and she jumped, instinct making her hit out as memories of a faceless attacker leapt into her mind.

Alex held her shoulders tight with hands that were browned by the sun. 'Don't turn your back on me, Natasha,' he said softly, and turned her to face him.

Her face was pale as she looked up at him, her eyes vivid in her skin. He still frightened her.

Alex studied her with a grim, unsmiling face.

'Still the same old Natasha,' he said flatly, his eyes intense. 'Tell me, do you have any other fears now? Have you gathered even more on the way? Or are you just the same neurotic child-woman I knew three years ago?'

If I have any other fears, she thought bitterly, staring up at him, it's because you implanted them. You're responsible this time, Alex, she thought, her eyes downcast, her lashes sweeping her cheeks. He saw too much, and she wasn't going to let him see the sudden flare of bitterness in her at his words.

He watched her for a moment in silence. 'Are you still in touch with your aunt?' he asked, tilting his black head to one side.

She nodded, avoiding his eyes. 'In a way,' she said huskily.

Alex nodded briefly, his eyes studying her assessingly. 'You're on Christmas card terms?' he stated without amusement.

He saw everything. If I'm such a good actress, Natasha thought with wild humour, why does he see through me so clearly? Why can he read my thoughts as easily as if they were his?

She looked up at him wearily. 'Why are you here, Alex?' she asked.

He watched her for a moment in silence, then a little smile curved his lips. He thrust his hands in his pockets, raising one brow as though trying to cover his thoughts. 'I thought we might have dinner together,' he told her wryly.

She shook her head. 'No—I'm sorry. I was planning on an evening on my own.' She looked up at him. 'I need time to get used to the idea of filming with you.' Perhaps honesty was the best course in a situation such as this.

He pursed his lips. 'At least you're honest,' he commented in a dry tone, his eyes teasing.

'Yes,' she said slowly, 'I've always been honest with you.'

They eyed each other silently for a few moments. Natasha knew what he was thinking, watching the frown which drew his black brows together over his arrogant nose.

'I don't think there's much point in going into that,' he said tightly.

She shrugged, hurt that he dismissed her words with such brutal ease. But what could she do but accept it? 'I agree,' she said quietly, 'so perhaps it's best if you just go.'

His mouth hardened into an angry line. 'Get dressed. We're going out for dinner.' His face was grim.

She shook her head. 'We're not. I'm not going anywhere with you.' It would be bad enough to work with him, without seeing him off the film set as well.

There was a little silence, then his mouth curled into a mocking smile, his old, cruel self taking over. 'I didn't ask you if you wanted to come,' he said unpleasantly, 'I just told you to get some clothes on.'

Her eyes flashed. 'I suppose you've even taken the precaution of booking a table for us?' she asked, feeling her temper rise at his arrogant assurance that she would drop everything and come running.

Alex inclined his head. 'We have a table for two at the Chantecler.' He laughed as he saw her outraged expression, and raised his hands to grip her shoulders, caressing them with his long fingers. 'It's only downstairs,' he drawled, 'so you needn't rush to make yourself beautiful for me.'

She shook herself free of his grasp, temper flaring inside her. He saw too damned much, he was too clever for her. He only had to take one look at her face to see what she was thinking.

'You take an awful lot for granted,' she said, her fists clenching at his tone. 'If you've been so stupid as to book a table for two, you're going to have a very lonely dinner!'

Alex laughed at her protests, his hands sliding slowly down her arms to caress her wrists. 'We could always have an intimate meal for two up here, if you'd prefer,' he murmured.

She tried to shake her wrists free, but his fingers tightened on them. 'Let me go,' she said shakily, suddenly very conscious of the look in those narrowed eyes.

He held her wrists with one hand, while the other hand moved to her breasts, one finger sliding along the line of the towel against her skin.

'My dear,' he drawled, his gaze insolent, 'I get the feeling you don't like me very much.'

Her pink mouth tightened. 'I despise you!' she said, her eyes flashing with distaste.

There was a short silence. He watched her intently, and she knew his mind was ticking over, wondering how he could best punish her for that statement.

Suddenly he pushed her against the wall, pinioning her hands high above her head. She gasped, trying to twist away from him, but he was too strong for her.

His gaze travelled over her body. 'I think,' he said slowly, 'you would look far more beautiful without this . . .'

She gasped as his hands suddenly flicked the towel away, leaving her naked, desperately trying to twist away from him so he couldn't see her.

Her cheeks flamed, her eyes stinging with tears of rage. 'Don't . . .!' she protested in breathless panic as he reached one hand towards her naked skin.

His lashes flicked against his tanned cheek and he looked back at her. 'I was right,' he said, his voice thickening, 'you are more beautiful without it.'

Natasha closed her eyes in momentary disbelief, 'You bastard!' she whispered through dry lips, her body still twisting away from him. 'Why won't you leave me alone?'

He laughed under his breath. 'Leave you alone?' he queried, a muscle jerking in his cheek as he slowly pressed against her. 'My dear, you're far too lovely for me to stay away from you.'

Her throat tightened as she felt the long cool fingers splay over her bare breast.

'You see?' Alex said thickly. 'You like it too.' His finger traced the outline of her hardening nipple and she gasped from deep in her throat. She could feel his long, lean legs pressing against her, their smooth feel encased in black trousers making her heart thud wildly.

'That's all I ever was to you, isn't it?' she breathed, her tone bitter, 'all I ever will be.'

There was a silence. Alex was watching her strangely, the words taking effect as he tightened his mouth into a firm straight line.

Natasha waited for a long time for him to reply, her breathing unsteady as her ears strained in the tense silence. Why was he so silent? Why didn't he answer her?

He turned away with a controlled expression on his face, and picked up the discarded bath towel. He handed it back to her, his face unsmiling, totally unreadable.

'Get dressed,' he said tightly. 'I'll wait for you downstairs.' He turned to leave the room, but stopped and came back, picking up the door key from the bed.

Natasha watched with a sinking heart. She had hoped he would leave it there.

He threw it up in his hand, caught it and put it in his pocket. 'I'll keep this,' he said, his mouth drawing into a tight, mocking smile. 'Be downstairs in the bar in fifteen minutes.'

He turned on his heel and left the room, closing it behind him with a sharp click.

Natasha stood quite still for a second, then stumbled over to the bed and collapsed on it, fighting back the tears. She had known for so long that he hated her, but it was difficult to face it when he was in the same room as her.

She dressed quickly, discarding her white lace

for the evening, knowing it would only bring more biting remarks from Alex on the subject of her image. Instead, she chose a simple red-gold coloured dress which fitted tightly around her breasts but flared at the hips. A complete contrast, she thought with a smile as she looked in the mirror.

The lift was crowded, and Natasha found herself squashed between three matronly Frenchwomen who reeked of expensive perfume and couture house silks.

Alex was waiting in the bar, seated opposite the piano-player, his gaze on the door. He inclined his head as she walked in and went to his table.

'You only just made it,' he drawled in her ear as he held her chair out for her to sit down. 'I was about to come up and help you dress.'

She bit her lip, avoiding his eyes. A waiter came buzzing over in a white dinner jacket and black tie, and took her order.

Alex gave her a mocking smile. 'I shouldn't have any wine,' he advised, and Natasha flushed angrily, her eyes hating him.

The piano-player smiled at her across the room and began playing 'As Time Goes By,' nodding at her to indicate that it was being played for her. She smiled back at him, grateful for at least one friendly face amidst the hostility directed from Alex.

Alex's watchful gaze didn't miss a trick. 'You appear to have found an admirer,' he said in a strangely flat voice as he studied her. 'I hope you won't get too friendly with the domestics.'

She looked at him irritably. 'Don't be so ridiculous! He was only being friendly.' Her fingers plucked restlessly with the skirt of her dress, smoothing the folds down.

Alex gave a harsh laugh. 'I always said you were naïve.' He watched as the waiter brought her drink, putting it smoothly on the table with a little bowl of peanuts and a plate of olives. The waiter gave her a broad smile, which disappeared when he caught Alex's eye.

'Thank you,' said Natasha, defiantly smiling back at the poor man, who had only been doing his job, which included being nice to the patrons of his bar.

When the waiter had left, Alex asked her, 'Do you mark each one down in your diary? Or do you just forget them?' He watched her over the brim of his glass, his face unsmiling.

She sighed, picking up the long iced drink and sipping it through the straws. She had only been polite to the man, why did Alex have to put the wrong construction on her actions?

They went in to dinner at just before eight o'clock. Natasha felt very detached as she walked along beside Alex, noticing the covetous glances thrown in his direction.

Women always looked at Alex Brent like that—and not because he was famous. His lean, hard body held a menacing sexuality, an implicit threat of sexual violence which attracted women like iron filings to a magnet. A good way to describe him, she thought with a little smile—he is magnetic.

They were seated at a table by the window, and

through the fine lace curtains they watched night-time Nice pass by.

Alex watched her through half closed lids as he leaned back in his seat. 'Are you looking forward to filming?' he asked.

She shrugged, not quite daring to tell him how much it scared her. Being with him day after day for months on end would play havoc with her nerves.

'Don't knock me over with enthusiasm,' he said drily, his hand closing over the long stem of his wine glass.

'Of course I'm looking forward to it,' she lied, resting her head on her clasped hands. 'It's an exciting script.'

The black eyes mocked her. 'Very,' he drawled, making his meaning crystal clear as a smile hovered around his firm lips.

Natasha looked away, willing the waiter to appear with their main course. As if by magic, their dinner came wheeling towards them on a long table, while waiters hovered nearby, silver dishes in their hands.

When their dinner was served, she began to eat the beautifully cooked steak, her eyes down, avoiding Alex's gaze.

She frowned as one of her potatoes collapsed. 'Oh dear,' she said with a sudden return of humour, 'I think something's happened to my potato.'

Alex smiled. 'It's just the skin,' he explained, looking over at her plate. 'You don't get the rest of it. God knows why—perhaps they consider it more genteel.'

Natasha returned his smile and their eyes met. They looked at each other for a long moment, and she felt her pulses quicken.

'Your eyes remind me of sapphires,' he said softly into the stillness between them. 'Did I ever tell you that?'

Natasha's breath caught in her throat at the sudden change of mood. 'Thank you,' she whispered, her eyes riveted on his across the flickering candle-flame.

There was another silence, then he said in a soft, urgent voice, 'Natasha . . .'

But before he could finish, she looked away in sudden confusion and picked up her wine glass, drinking far too much far too quickly.

Alex was watching her with narrowed, intent eyes. She put the glass down and carried on with her meal, but her appetite had gone, and inside her stomach, little butterflies of excitement and fear made her feel sick every time she looked at her food.

After dinner he insisted on taking her back to her room. She turned worried eyes on him as they waited for the lift behind the marble pillars.

'I must get to sleep straightaway,' she told him, 'I have to be up early tomorrow.'

He raised one dark brow as he looked down at her. 'Really?' he queried with evident disbelief, 'What for?'

She looked down at her hands as they stepped into the lift. Alex pressed the button for her floor and leaned lazily against the wall as it moved upwards.

'I wanted to read the script, do some shopping and spend some time on the beach,' she said, trying to think of everything possible and cram it all into one day.

He laughed under his breath. 'Try again, my darling. I can spot a lie a mile off.' He took her arm as they reached her floor and began to walk down the corridor with her. 'I was told you were an excellent actress. You must be losing your touch.'

She tightened her lips, but said nothing in reply. Alex unlocked her door and reached one hand out to flick on the light. She turned in the doorway to face him,

'Thank you for the dinner,' she said with a nervous smile, 'I enjoyed it very much.' She held her breath, hoping he would go away.

He leaned forward and captured her chin with one sinewy hand, caressing it softly. 'How much?' he murmured.

Natasha moistened her lips with her tongue. 'I don't understand what you mean,' she said nervously, not daring to pull away in case she angered him and incited him into following her into the room.

'It's quite simple,' he said, his gaze glittering on her face, 'I asked how much you enjoyed our evening together.'

She frowned, a definite sense of unease building up inside her. 'I told you,' she said shortly, unable to help herself as her pulses skipped with confusion.

Alex watched her for a moment in silence, his

long fingers still against her chin. Then he softly began caressing her skin again, his head tilting to one side.

'When I was much younger,' he said softly, 'my girl-friends used to give me a goodnight kiss after I'd taken them out.'

Natasha swallowed. Slowly she stood on tiptoe until her face was next to his, and brushed her lips against his. Her heart skipped a beat at the look in his eyes as their mouths touched.

'Goodnight,' she whispered breathlessly.

His hand didn't leave her face. 'But now that I'm older,' he said huskily, 'my girl-friends take me to their beds.'

She whitened visibly and pulled away from him, trying to shut the door in his face, frightened that he would make her go to bed with him.

He moved to the door, kicking it back, and she shrank against the wall, breathing hard, her eyes wide and startled as he looked at her.

'Leave me alone!' she whispered, putting her hands up as he came towards her with an angry, set expression.

He took her arms and held her against the wall. 'Why did you shut the door on my face?' he asked bitingly, his mouth hard and angry.

She stared up at him, alarmed. 'Because . . .' she began, swallowing hard, 'because you said that . . .'

His eyes flashed with temper, his hands biting into her arms. 'It was a joke, damn you,' he bit out, 'a joke! Or have you lost your sense of humour as well as your reason?'

She flushed hotly, fear leaping into her throat as she stared up at him in the tense, angry silence that followed.

Suddenly he released her with a thrust, and his eyes flicked over her. 'You're not worth the effort!' he said with disgust, and turned on his heel, walking out of her room and slamming the door behind him.

Natasha looked down at the floor, tears blurring her eyes. He had said the very same words to her three years ago, and she had cried just as painfully as she did now.

He had arrived back from Italy, his flight delayed by three hours, stopping Natasha reaching him at the airport. But Roger had not been so easily put off. Roger Brent, Alex's young brother, had gone up to meet him at the airport.

Alex had stormed into their home an hour after his flight landed and burst into Natasha's bedroom.

'Is it true?' he had demanded, his face flooding with so many emotions that she could only stare at him in bewilderment.

'Is what true, darling?' she had asked, frowning, concerned at the pained expression on his face. She had taken three steps towards him, ready to put her arms round him, comfort him.

But his icy voice had stopped her. 'Did you sleep with my brother?' he demanded bitingly, and her heart had frozen in horror.

She had stared in amazement and disbelief. 'No!'

She had laughed nervously in her disbelief, thinking that perhaps it was a joke. 'Don't be silly, of course I didn't!'

His eyes had blazed with rage. 'Don't lie to me!' he had shouted angrily, his fists clenching and un-clenching at his sides.

She had been almost incoherent in her shock, staring at him with horrified eyes, her body rushing with fear, panic, anger. 'I don't understand, Alex. Who told you such a thing?'

Conflict raged in his eyes, and he reached out to her. 'Natasha . . .' he said on a groan of physical pain, 'tell me it isn't true, tell me he's lying!'

She went into his arms, looking up into his face. 'Who's lying? Tell me who said it, Alex!' Her heart was thudding crazily as she tried to figure out what was going on.

'Roger. He said . . .' Alex broke off roughly, his voice choking as he gripped her shoulder with biting fingers. 'Is it true?'

She had shaken her head, her frown etched with pain and worry. 'No,' she said quietly. 'No, it isn't true.'

Alex groaned in painful relief, taking her in his arms and stroking her hair while she clung on to him for all she was worth. I have an enemy, she realised bitterly as she caught sight of Roger watching sulkily from the doorway.

Oh yes, she thought now, staring out at Nice enveloped in darkness, I had an enemy all right. It had taken him only an hour more to split them up completely.

But Natasha couldn't go back that far, because

it hurt too much. Slowly, she crawled into bed and waited for dawn.

The telephone woke her at eleven. Natasha looked up, blinking the sleep from her eyes. Her breakfast had been brought in and left uneaten. She groaned, wondering what time she had eventually fallen asleep.

Reaching for the receiver, she fumbled for it before eventually lifting it to her ear. 'Hello?' she said wearily.

A Frenchwoman did her best to speak English as she said; 'I 'ave a call for the money to be paid by you, *mademoiselle*. Will you pay for eet?'

Natasha frowned, rolling over on to her back and stretching her aching shoulders. 'Where is it from?' she asked, gathering that it was a reversed-charge call.

'Oh, I am sorry,' the woman said with a smile in her voice. 'Eet ees from London, England.'

'Tasha?' Her aunt's raucous cockney accent crackled along the line and Natasha winced at the horrible sound of her name from the woman's lips.

'Hello, Aunt Stella,' she said warily, wondering what she wanted. 'How are you?'

'Oh, not so bad. Bin 'aving a bit of trouble with the pub—you know what it's like now that lot are back in government, what with their taxes an' all.' Her aunt's voice was marred slightly by the fact that the cigarette that dangled permanently from her red mouth got in the way of her conversation. 'Still, I mustn't complain.'

Natasha sighed. 'I'll send you a cheque next

week,' she promised, wishing there was some other way she could reply. But she couldn't go back there to help out. Not ever.

'Oh, thank you, you are a good girl!' Her aunt sounded jubilant. 'Now, what I rang for actually wasn't to ask you for money. It's a little delicate, which is why I thought to myself—best ring her now and 'ave done with it.'

Natasha frowned. What was she getting at? 'Delicate?' she asked worriedly.

'Well,' confided Stella, her voice lowering to an excited hush, 'you'll never guess who came 'ere looking for you the other day. It was that Roger Brent—you know, Alex's brother.'

Natasha's heart stopped on a lurch of panic. 'Did . . . did he say what he wanted?' she asked, her eyes widening as she sat up to listen properly.

'No,' her aunt said disappointedly, 'wouldn't say what he wanted, just asked if I'd seen you. I said no, my Tasha don't come home much no more. Too busy going round the world being famous.' There was a trace of bitter envy in her voice.

Natasha suddenly felt sorry for her, and resolved to send her a larger amount than usual. They talked for a few more minutes.

When her aunt had hung up, Natasha replaced the receiver, feeling very ill at ease. She sat in bed, wondering what on earth Roger had wanted to see her about.

Not that she would have seen him, of course. She felt too much anger towards him to ever speak to him again. But it was worrying all the same that he should reappear at the same time as Alex.

She went over to the writing desk by the window and wrote out a large cheque for her aunt. Then she quickly wrote a little note for her and slipped it in the envelope.

Natasha had lived with her aunt between the ages of twelve and eighteen. Her parents had been killed in a terrible car crash just before her tweflth birthday, and after that, her whole world had crumbled to dust around her.

Natasha Fox had been born into a beautiful paradise, filled with elegant smiling women and handsome well-dressed men. Her earliest memory was that of her mother bending over her white lace cradle, her beautiful face filled with kindness, her soft voice like music on a breeze. Her silver bracelets had jangled softly as she reached out to pick Natasha up and hold her next to her, where Natasha had smelt her mother's exquisite flowery perfume and tangled her tiny fingers with wonder in her hair.

Her parents had married for love in a world where love counted for everything. Her father had been a dark, smiling figure with jet black hair and kind eyes, towering over her like an illusion while her mother leant on his arm. Theirs had been a marriage built on a fairytale world where nothing was real, and everything was beautiful.

Natasha's life between the ages of nought to twelve was spent in this paradise, and she saw the world through a veil of sunny afternoons, soft laughter and long warm days filled with pleasure.

Then her parents' car had crashed, and the glass palace came crashing down around her ears. She had been cast out of the paradise and straight into reality. Her father had died leaving a string of unpaid bills. The estate was sold, Natasha's clothes were sold, her exquisitely beautiful toys were sold and Natasha was left with nothing but memories.

Her aunt, Stella Jenkins, lived in a dirty little house in Whitechapel, in the heart of London's East End. She had been ostracised by the family since she was sixteen, for getting pregnant by a docker in Millwall.

Penniless and alone, Stella had married the strong-armed docker and moved to Whitechapel, where she had lived for the rest of her life. She was bitter, her world a living hell, and to make up for it she became even more promiscuous, spending her time and what little money she had in the local pubs, going home with any man who so much as smiled at her.

This then was the world into which Natasha was forced. As she grew up and the promise of her beauty was fulfilled, so Stella became more harsh with her, envy making her spiteful. Stella's boy-friends were becoming increasingly watchful of Natasha, their greedy eyes following her when Stella brought them home.

When she was sixteen, one of Stella's boy-friends made a pass at her. He came up behind her in her bedroom and slid his arms round her, his hands sliding on to her forming breasts. Natasha had screamed, spinning round in panic, her eyes wild as she hit out at him, arms flailing. The man had pushed her on to the bed, his eyes filled with lust and greed.

Stella had fortunately arrived back from the shops at that moment. She had thrown the man out of the house, blaming Natasha afterwards for what had happened, calling her a prococious little slut.

Natasha had pushed the incident to the back of her mind. But from then on, whenever someone came up behind her too close, something would snap in her head and she would react unconsciously, her subconscious pushing her into violent reaction.

When she was eighteen, she auditioned at a drama school, and it was there that she met Alex Brent. He had agreed to audition one of the afternoon's load of hopeful actors and actresses. Everyone had recognised him, of course—his face was world-famous.

When it was Natasha's turn, she had gone into the room, her nerves making her shake. Alex Brent had looked up and stared at her, his eyes eating her while she performed. He hadn't said a word, just stared at her for the whole course of her audition.

Afterwards, she had been accepted to the school, and called back by Alex. From then on, they were inseparable. They were with each other every night, locked in the fascination and intensity of a powerful attraction.

They had been married six months later, and Natasha left her aunt's home with mixed feelings of joy and guilt. She had refused to allow Alex to help her career by coupling his name too openly with hers. Their marriage had been kept a total secret. Nobody had known. Except Roger . . .

After she had got dressed there was a knock on the door. She went towards it, her eyes narrowed with suspicion. 'Who is it?' she called, her heart beating a little too fast as she waited.

'Room Service, *mademoiselle*,' came the broken French reply.

She opened the door and peered round the corner. A huge basket of blood red roses confronted her. She opened the door wider and allowed the young man to walk in and put the roses down on her table.

'Thank you,' she said slowly as he went out, and went over to the roses to inspect them.

Nestling against the silver basket was a small envelope with her name on it. Alex, she thought, noting the strong black handwriting, and ripping open the envelope.

Her eyes scanned it quickly. 'I'll get you in the end, my darling,' it read. She closed her eyes and screwed it up violently in her hand, throwing it in the bin.

'Blood red . . .' she murmured under her breath, touching the soft petals of the roses. Clever, she thought, shivering.

She went downstairs, intending to do some shopping in Nice. But as she walked through the foyer, she heard someone call her name, and turned.

'*Une lettre pour vous*, Mademoiselle Fox!' The desk clerk waved it at her from reception.

She sighed. Who knew she was here? Her heart stopped—not Roger? Surely not? She opened the

letter with trembling hands and pulled it out, looking at the signature first. It was from Marney.

'. . . Be at the Carlton Hotel, Cannes, tonight for
a dinner party with the producer and a few friends.
Wear something sexy, there might be a couple
of reporters there.'

She sighed. Another evening without the peace
she craved so much! Still, she might get lonely if
she stayed in her hotel tonight—and there was
always the chance that Alex might try to get in her
room again.

After all, he still had the key.

CHAPTER THREE

SHE pulled up outside the Carlton at eight-thirty. The traffic had delayed her—that and finding a taxi at seven-forty-five on a Friday night in Nice. True to Marney's word, there was a crowd outside the hotel and Natasha had to fight her way through to the hotel, giving brief smiles to the men who photographed her as she walked.

She went into the lounge and sighed with relief as she saw a face she knew. 'Cara! Thank God you're here!' she exclaimed, going across the lounge. 'I thought I'd never get through that lot outside. What on earth were they all doing here?'

Cara Grey was also starring in the film. She was a tall, elegant woman with the style and sophistication of a veteran actress. At thirty-five years of age (or so she claimed!) she was still ravishing.

'Darling!' she smiled, her chestnut-coloured hair drawn in a severe ponytail off her classically beautiful face with enormous dark wells of brown eyes. 'We thought you'd never get here!'

Natasha smiled with genuine warmth. Cara was a good friend, even though she was twelve years older than Natasha. 'The traffic was murderous. I had to practically stand in the middle of the road and hitch my skirt up to get a taxi!'

Cara laughed earthily, her voice like dark, throaty velvet. 'You should marry a sexy chauffeur like I did!' She looked round mischievously, 'Only don't tell him I said that. Judd has a very sensitive ego – he prefers to be referred to as a business man, even if he does drive me around.'

Natasha allowed herself to be led away by the older woman. 'Is everyone else here?' she asked as they walked towards the private dining room.

Cara raised a dark, expertly plucked brow. 'You could say that!' she said, amused. Secret laughter filled her dark eyes as she pushed the doors of the dining room open. Applause burst out and Natasha looked on in amazement at the entire film set of *The Devil's Mistress*.

'Cara . . .' she said ruefully, giving her a grudging smile, 'I thought Marney said it was just a few friends?'

Cara laughed, her elegant shoulders rippling. 'Let's not quibble over minor details.'

Natasha grinned. 'Why not?'

'That's what I like about you,' said Cara drily, 'you're so spontaneous!'

At that moment B.B. Jackson stood up on a raised platform and began making a speech. 'I know that with our combined love and effort we will make this a motion picture to exceed all others,' he began.

Cara wiped her eyes with exaggeration. 'He's breaking my heart,' she drawled, grinning at Natasha. Across the room someone started playing an imaginary violin. 'Do you believe this?' Cara asked Natasha as they made their way to their table.

Natasha stifled a giggle. 'Sssh! He'll hear you.'

She looked round fondly at B.B. on the stage. 'I think he's sweet.'

'The man's a living saint,' Cara drawled. 'Throw him a halo.'

Natasha suddenly stiffened as she saw a face through the crowd. His lids were half lowered against cigar smoke as he watched her, his mouth straight and controlled. He inclined his head in a gesture of acknowledgement.

How could she be so stupid? Of course Alex would be here. Everyone else who was involved on the production was in the room, so it followed that Alex would be there too.

'Where are we sitting?' she asked worriedly. They seemed to be making their way to Alex's table, and she had no wish to sit with him all night.

Cara pointed with long elegant fingers. 'Over there.'

Natasha's heart nosedived into her boots. It was Alex's table all right. But that was another show of her stupidity—she should have realised they would automatically put the leading actors together.

Her heart thudded fast as she walked on weak legs to her table. Alex stood up, watching her with ironic eyes.

'Hello, Natasha,' he murmured, amusement in his voice as he held her chair out for her.

She avoided his gaze, her lashes sweeping her cheeks. 'Hello,' she said calmly, trying to control her leaping pulses.

'Hello, Alex,' said Cara warmly, brushing her smooth cheek against his and smiling at him, her red lips curling upwards. She jerked her head in the direction of B.B., who was still droning away. 'It looks like one hell of an evening,' she said drily.

Alex laughed, sitting down next to Natasha and handing her a Martini. He picked up his own drink and held it to his lips, watching her over the brim of the glass.

'You're late,' he murmured so that no one else could hear. 'What kept you? Or should I say, who kept you?' One jet black brow was raised as he spoke.

Natasha looked away, compressing her lips. He was starting early tonight! He seemed to attack her every step of the way, and she only wished she could do something to stop him. But common sense dictated that to try to argue with him would cause her trouble, and she could well do without that.

Dinner was served quickly, and they sat back and watched with amazement as the plates were piled high. There were four courses in all, beginning with pâté de foie gras, which was mouthwateringly delicious, melting on the tongue.

'This makes me feel ill,' Cara commented as she pushed her plate away leaving it virtually untouched. 'The way they fatten those poor geese up and wait like spiders for them to die is sick-making!' She flicked her napkin over the plate with distaste. 'There,' she said, hiding the food beneath the damask cloth, 'you can hide where I can't see you.'

Natasha grimaced, but refused to be put off. Cara smoked restlessly throughout the first and second courses, ignoring the fish which was put in front of her and blowing smoke out of the corner of her red mouth as she looked away from the table.

'Do you never eat?' Alex asked with amusement, a smile curving his mouth. He watched Cara as she finished her meat course, eating only half of it before pushing the plate away abruptly and lighting another cigarette.

'I eat like a pig,' she said drily, raising a brow and blowing smoke out of the corner of her mouth. 'That's why I can't let myself get interested in the food. I'd end up looking like Mount Vesuvius on a bad day, and my career would go down the chute.'

Coffee was served at last and Natasha sipped the hot drink far too quickly. She scalded her tongue, jumping a little, and putting the cup down on the saucer.

Alex was watching her. 'Scalded yourself again, Natasha?' he enquired coolly, his message coming across loud and clear. 'You seem to make a habit of that.' And his mouth curved with amusement, his black eyes glinting at her.

She flushed, her hands plucking restlessly at the tablecloth. 'I didn't realise how hot it was,' she replied.

'No,' he agreed ironically, 'you never do.'

Natasha looked away from him, avoiding his intense gaze. The band in the corner of the room started to play, their shiny black dinner jackets reflecting the light as they broke into music. B.B. Jackson wobbled over to the raised platform in the centre of the room, smoking a fat cigar and patting people on the back as he went.

'Ladies and gentlemen,' he said, his hands resting

on his large stomach, which seemed to have grown considerably over dinner, 'I'm sure we'd all like nothing better than to start the dancing. And who better to do that than our two stars?' His eyes gleamed as he looked over at their table. 'Sabrina and Lynx!' he announced, starting to clap them happily.

Natasha looked up in dismay. She couldn't possibly dance with Alex, not after what had been said in their argument last night. But she should have realised that they would be expected to dance together. They were the main attraction of the film.

'Come along, my dear,' Alex drawled, standing up and drawing her chair back for her, 'they're waiting for us.' His body was close to hers as she stood up, and she turned her head, looking up into his mocking eyes. It was so unfair to have to go through with this charade. Nobody knew of the violent undercurrents running between them. No one knew what had happened between them.

Alex curled one hand possessively on her arm and led her to the dance floor amid the applause and glittering lights. His hands slid round her waist as he drew her towards him. 'You still dance beautifully,' he murmured in her ear as they danced languorously.

'Thank you,' she replied, confusion running through her at his gentle approach. His hands slid down her back to her hips, caressing them sensually, making her skin flush with confusion and half excitement. 'Don't, Alex!' she snapped irritably, pushing his hands away from her body.

Alex smiled wickedly at her, his hands sliding up towards her breasts, and she broke away from him, a frown on her face. 'Alex . . .' she began in a breathless voice.

'People are staring,' Alex cut in before she could finish, and he jerked her back against him, his lazy smile making the hair on the back of her neck prickle.

She looked away from him, angry at being trapped in her own web of lies. 'They're staring because you keep touching me,' she told him, brushing his hands away from her hips.

The music played on, and Natasha and Alex moved sensually round the dance floor alone. No one else danced, and the spotlight fell on them as they moved together. Her hair glistened like spun gold in the white moon of the spotlight, the explosive combination of her fragile beauty and golden hair a perfect foil for his dark Satanic good looks. Everyone's eyes were on them, noting the way their bodies moved as one, sliding against each other on the dance floor.

When the music stopped there was a loud burst of applause, and Alex held on tight to Natasha's wrist, forcing her to stay with him and take a bow next to him.

As the applause died away, and people began to dance as well, Natasha tried to turn and walk back to their table.

'Not so fast,' Alex drawled in her ear, pulling her back to him. 'I want a little word with you.'

She eyed him suspiciously, her eyes fixing on his face. 'You can talk to me here, can't you?'

He grimaced. 'Unfortunately, no.' He took her arm and lead her off the dance floor in the direction of the door. Natasha walked by his side, not wishing to incur the curious glances of others in the room by arguing with him. She frowned as she looked at the back of his black head, wondering what he was up to.

Alex closed the door behind them and lounged casually against the wall in the empty, silent corridor. Natasha felt herself become rather nervous, her eyes avoiding his as she bit her lip, aware that they were now totally alone once more.

His eyes flicked slowly over her. 'Did I tell you how lovely you look tonight?' he asked softly.

Natasha looked up. 'No,' she said in a dry tone. 'And I'm flattered, but I don't really see what that has to do with why you want to talk to me.' She tried to guess at the thoughts inside that clever head, but his face was an impenetrable mask.

Alex slid one hand in his pocket, examining the long fingers of his other hand with apparent interest. 'I understand Roger paid a visit to your aunt's house the other day,' he said casually.

She caught her breath, staring at him wide-eyed. 'How did you know?' she breathed, her mind working overtime. She herself had only heard from Aunt Stella that morning, so it followed that Roger must have been in touch with him. There was no other way he could possibly know about it.

'I heard from Roger this morning,' Alex said flatly, confirming her thoughts.

She bent her head. Dear God, she thought with

anguish, will he never let me rest? She put a hand against her suddenly hot cheeks, trying to cool them. 'What did he say?' she asked.

Alex watched her intensely. 'Very little, as a matter of fact. He did ask me to wish you luck with the film, though.' His mouth hardened a little and his voice became an unpleasant drawl. 'I expect he still has a soft spot for you.'

She looked up, her face angry. 'It isn't reciprocated, believe me,' she said between her teeth. No way, she thought. If I ever set eyes on Roger again I think I might kill him!

The black eyes narrowed. 'Just a passing fancy, was he?' he asked in a mocking drawl.

Natasha closed her eyes for a moment. She was afraid she might lose her temper if they spoke about his brother too much. His name could still invoke bitterness. 'I don't want to talk about it any more,' she said in a stiff voice. 'Can we discuss something else?'

'No, we can't,' he said, studying her with an angry expression. He pushed away from the wall and took a step towards her, towering over her like a dangerous shadow waiting to envelop her in eternal darkness. 'I want to know if you're still seeing him. I can't expect him to tell me, but I'll force it out of you if I have to.'

She felt her temper shoot out of sight. After all the pain she had been through at his hands, she couldn't forgive him for asking such a stupid, insulting question.

'I thought you knew everything,' she said angrily, her eyes hating him for believing such a thing of her. 'You should at least know the answer to that question.'

Alex took her wrist with biting fingers. 'Funny!' he snapped, his black eyes flashing with temper. He raked one hand through his hair, looking down at her with an angry expression. 'Am I supposed to laugh?' He raised one dark brow.

'Do what you like.'

His gaze fastened on her mouth. 'Is that an invitation?' he drawled tightly, his voice thickening as his gaze flickered down over her body, resting on her breasts before flicking back up to her now flushed face.

Natasha felt her heart thump faster as a warning signal. Alex was in a dangerous mood and she wanted no part of it. His call from Roger had obviously made him angry, and now he was directing that anger towards her.

She tried to control herself, standing at her full height and meeting his eyes calmly. 'Is that all?' she asked in a quiet voice, not wanting to arouse his temper. 'Can I go now?'

'Oh no,' he answered unpleasantly, his thumb caressing her wrist. 'I have more news for you.' He paused, and the black eyes burned into her. 'They want us to do all the sex scenes in the film—no doubles.'

Her eyes widened in disbelief. It was written into her contract that she would not have to appear in front of the cameras even partially unclothed. He must be lying to her. 'I think you're mistaken,' she said, choosing her words carefully.

A lazy smile curved his mouth. 'No,' he disagreed, shaking his head slowly. 'They want me to take all your clothes off and make love to you.'

Natasha whitened, her blue eyes vivid against her skin. He couldn't be serious! Yet that deep voice carried a ring of conviction that was hard to disbelieve. She had made it plain that she would do no sex scenes. She never had done any. But above all, she couldn't do it with Alex. The thought of it made her shiver.

'I don't believe you!' she said in a low angry voice, shaking her head.

He laughed huskily under his breath as she tried to pull away from him. His hands caught hers easily, and he twisted them behind her, pulling her towards him so she pressed against him, her breasts pushing out against his chest.

'Why not?' he asked, one dark brow raised. 'I'm sure you'll enjoy doing them immensely. I know I will.' His gaze darkened, his thighs pressing against hers. 'I find the idea very exciting.'

Her lips tightened. 'You bastard!' she said in a whisper of anger, distaste flashing in her blue eyes. 'You know damn well I don't want anything to do with you!'

As though her reply hurt him, his face tightened into a grim unsmiling mask, and he pushed her roughly against the wall, holding her still with controlled power. 'I'm sure you don't, my dear,' he said unpleasantly, and his hands hurt her, 'but you do seem to enjoy my touch.'

She stared at him in a confusion of hatred and excitement. How can he hurt me this way, she thought, after all he's done in the past? She looked quickly up and down the corridor for help, a face she knew. But it was deserted.

'I won't do it, Alex,' she said in a low voice. 'I'll see you in hell before I let you into my bed—on screen or off!'

There was a tense silence. 'My darling,' he said thickly, 'I'd put you through hell now if I thought it would do me any good.' She tried to twist away from him while he was still, but her movements angered him and he thrust her back against the wall without mercy, his eyes glittering like chips of polished jet.

His black head lowered slowly, his hard mouth brushing against her lips in coaxing, sensual movements, and she caught her breath, trying desperately to resist his touch.

'Stop it!' she whispered, twisting her head away from him, struggling uselessly against him. He tightened his fingers on her wrists and she stood still, not wanting to feel any more physical pain.

His mouth teased hers exquisitely. 'Would you like to go to hell with me, my sweet?' he asked, and her heart began thudding violently. His mouth closed over hers, passion flaring between them. Her body gave in to the slow torturing ecstasy of his kiss, leaving her mind screaming soundlessly. She couldn't resist his overwhelming sexuality as he kissed her, his hands imprisoning hers.

His mouth blazed a trail to her neck, his sharp white teeth nibbling and biting at her soft skin, and she moaned, twisting her head from side to side, her mind trying to take control.

His tongue snaked out across her throat, and

her pulses skidded crazily, her body shivering. He looked up at her for a moment, his black eyes shrewd as they took in the confused state she was in.

A sweet rush of excitement filled her as his mouth moved lazily to kiss the shivering white skin of her breasts which rose and fell with her laboured breathing.

'Don't . . .' she whispered in breathless confusion, her body writhing away from his, and he stopped kissing her for a moment, leaving her breathing unsteadily to look down at him.

He looked up, the black lashes flickering against his tanned cheek. 'Don't you like it?' he asked, his black eyes mocking her, a slow smile curving his mouth.

Her mouth compressed angrily. 'No!' she said, fiercely denying it, angry with herself for having allowed him to touch her. Dear God, she thought, closing her eyes, why does he have this effect on me? Why do I find him so damned irresistible?

The door behind them opened, and Alex raised his head, his eyes narrowing. A waiter eyed them with professional, bland indifference and walked silently down the corridor.

Natasha tried to break away from him, her breathing unsteady. She kept her face tautly controlled as she looked at him. 'We have nothing more to say to each other, Alex.'

He raised his brows. 'Is that so?' he murmured, his eyes skimming over her. He reached out lazily and pulled her towards him. 'I must disagree. We have far too much to say to each other.' He gave her a slow smile.

Natasha's eyes followed the waiter helplessly. If only she had called out to him, asked for help when he came out of the dining room. Why hadn't she been quick enough to do that? But she knew that if she had done so Alex would have been furious with her.

She looked back at Alex as the waiter disappeared around the corner. 'I'm not interested in anything you have to say,' she told him, trying to hide her nervousness behind a shield of indifference.

Alex's eyes narrowed, his mouth tightening. He took her chin with one hand, thrusting her head up to look at him, and pressed the smooth skin below her chin with his thumb, caressing her cheek with one long index finger.

'Aren't you?' he asked in a drawl, but she could see she had stung him with her reply. 'I don't believe you, Natasha. You're not indifferent to me, any more than I am to you.'

She flushed, her teeth clamping together. Why was he so shrewd, so clever? Trying to fight him was like trying to fight a razor blade. He sliced you in two every time.

'You're wrong,' she said angrily, trying to bluff her way out of it. She looked him straight in the eye, gathering all her courage. 'I am indifferent to you. You leave me cold!'

He raised his brows, inclining his black head as he watched her. 'Is that so?' he said tightly, still not put off by her words. 'If you were indifferent to me, my dear, you would feel nothing for me. But you respond with such delightful abandon when I kiss you. And you seem to hate me so excitingly.'

She flushed, her temper getting the better of her. 'Any woman with her head screwed on would get angry if you didn't keep your hands to yourself!' she snapped, determined not to lose this argument.

A tide of deep red flowed up his neck, staining the skin beneath his tan. A muscle jerked in his cheek as he watched her, and the silence was tense, throbbing with danger.

Then she felt his hands slide slowly up her neck to grasp a handful of her hair, twisting it slowly around his fingers. He pulled her head back in a gentle movement, looking down into her face with calculating eyes.

His gaze was narrowed, intent. He leaned forwards, his lips brushing hers again. He kissed her deeply, his mouth changing from sensual coaxing to ruthless persuasion. Natasha ignored his touch, remaining calm. When he lifted his head to look down at her she said,

'You see? You leave me cold.' And she looked at him with raised brows, her face impassive.

'You little bitch!' he muttered, his skin flushing with colour. 'We'll soon see if you're the ice maiden you pretend to be!' and he took her arm, dragging her off down the corridor without a backward glance.

Alarmed, she stumbled after him, her heart thudding as he pulled her down the long corridor. Now what have I got myself into? she thought bitterly. I shouldn't have argued with him, I should have kept my temper in check. But that wasn't fair to herself, and she knew it. Why should she let herself be bullied by him?

'Stop, Alex,' she begged, rushing along to keep up with his strides, almost stumbling over as they went into the foyer of the hotel.

'We're going home, my sweet,' he bit out unpleasantly, 'to test your indifference.' He threw her a mocking glance. 'We have a scene to rehearse for the film!' and he laughed at her worried expression.

Then all hell broke loose around them. Bulbs flashed, people jostled, faces pushing up against them, shouting questions until Natasha's mind whirled. She clung to Alex as he pushed his way through, forcing people out of the way with an angry face.

They shouted questions in French, waving pads in the air, their faces eager and enquiring. Then a little man with piggy eyes pushed his face into theirs. 'Is it true that you once had an affair with Miss Fox?' he asked insolently. 'And are you still together?'

Alex looked at him with murderous eyes. His fist shot out and cracked the man on the jaw, sending him flying. A roar of horror went up from the crowd, but Alex ignored it, as he battled his way through.

Natasha crimsoned as they fought their way out. How had they found out? Who could have told them about her and Alex? It had all been so long ago.

As they reached the marble steps outside, she felt herself stumble lost in her thoughts.

'Alex!' she cried, as she fell backwards.

He caught and held her in his arms, his black eyes glittering as he looked down into her upturned face, her blue eyes startled, her lips parted in surprise. Her golden hair spilled over his sleeve as they stared at each other with a rush of sudden emotion.

The flashbulbs popped furiously. That photograph became an international sensation. It was splashed over every magazine cover, posted on billboards all over Europe and the States. Their faces had shown the passion and intensity of Lynx and Sabrina, and people went crazy over it.

Alex pulled her to her feet and rushed her out to the car, pushing her inside and jumping in after her. The car screamed away, burning rubber on the road as it moved.

'How did they find out?' she asked him into the silence as they drove back along the coast to Nice.

He turned blazing eyes on her. 'I expect,' he said between his teeth, 'your friends leaked it to them for good publicity.'

She gasped, her brow creasing in a frown. 'Don't be ridiculous! My friends wouldn't do a thing like that.' Her mind darted crazily as she tried to think hard. Who could have told them? No one had known at the time they were together.

Suddenly she knew beyond all doubt who had told the press. 'Roger!' she said aloud, not realising she had spoken, her mind working too quickly to check herself.

Alex turned to look at her. 'Are you mad?' he

demanded angrily, his lip curling into a sneer. 'Why the hell should Roger tell them?'

She glared at him. Oh, she knew, all right. Roger had been the troublemaker all along. He had split them up. He had ruined her life for the past three years. She had thought she had found happiness after so long living in the grey world, then Roger had appeared on the scene, and smashed her chances as though they were crystals of glass.

Alex believed his brother, trusted him. He didn't believe in Natasha, and he didn't trust her very much either. It had been this way all along. Natasha was the woman he had loved, the woman who had shared so much with him, but he couldn't bring himself to believe in her over his brother.

Roger had been very young when Alex's mother died. She had begged Alex to look after her younger son, knowing how weak he was, knowing that Alex was stronger than he. Age had nothing to do with it. Roger had just been born with a weak mind, and Alex had had to take care of him. He had done what his mother asked him—right down to the letter.

They pulled up outside her hotel, and Alex pulled her out of the car. The marble floor echoed with their footsteps as they walked through the foyer to the lifts.

Natasha watched Alex worriedly out of the corner of her eyes as the lift sped upwards, and they got out at her floor. She walked beside him with a thumping heart and a knot of hard panic inside her.

He pushed her inside the room and flicked the

light on. 'Now,' he said between his teeth, 'we have a little debt to settle.'

She backed away from him, panic shining from her eyes. 'Please don't do this, Alex,' she whispered in an agonised tone. 'Please!'

As if her pleading aroused some emotion in him, he stopped, his face hardening momentarily. 'Very well,' he said flatly, 'we'll have a drink first, shall we? Perhaps it will make you more receptive.'

She swallowed, and closed her eyes. He really meant to go through with this. How could she stop him, how could she get away from him? She should have called someone downstairs in the lobby when they were there, but she had been too frightened of Alex's response.

He took a bottle of champagne from the fridge and uncorked it, pouring it into two crystal glasses. 'After all,' he said unpleasantly, 'I do prefer to take a responsive woman to my bed.'

She twisted her hands together to try to stop them shaking. 'I . . . I don't want any champagne,' she protested, her voice uncontrolled.

Alex raised one dark brow, his face tight. He walked slowly to where she stood and raised one glass. 'Here,' he said, dipping one long finger in the champagne, 'try just a little.'

Her pulses leapt as he offered her his finger, moistening her lips with the wetness from the drink. She stared at him with wide eyes as he watched her tongue dart out to lick her lips free.

'Do you want some more?' he asked thickly, his eyes following the movement intensely.

'No!' she whispered in breathless panic, her

pulses skidding crazily. She swallowed on a tight knot of fear. 'Alex, I just want to be left alone.'

He laughed huskily. 'That's a cliché, my darling,' he said, putting one of the glasses down on top of the fridge. 'It's been used far too often.'

He came back to where she stood, his hand reaching out to grasp a handful of her silky golden hair. 'Your hair has always fascinated me,' he told her in a husky voice. 'I like to tangle it in my fingers when we make love.'

Her heart skidded to a stop, then burst back into life, and she closed her eyes. 'That was all over a long time ago,' she reminded him bitterly. 'It's finished. You didn't want me then and there's no way you're getting me now.'

'How wrong you are, my sweet,' he said mockingly, his eyes blazing into hers. 'I wanted you very much—don't you remember?' His hand jerked her head back, and he laughed harshly. 'I was even fool enough to marry you to get what I wanted!'

Natasha looked away. 'Yes,' she said with painful bitterness, 'but not enough to tell anyone except your dear brother that we were married!' She felt her fists clench with anger at the memory.

'I'll make up for it now, shall I?' he drawled mockingly. 'I'll tell everyone just how married we are.' He looked down at her and his mouth curved in a smile.

She looked at him sharply, unsure as to whether or not he meant it. No, she decided, studying his hard-boned face, he would no more tell the press than she would. They both wanted to keep it a secret, but no one more than Natasha. I couldn't bear it if everyone knew, she thought, looking away from him. They would all watch her with prying, curious eyes, ready to see her fall into Alex's arms without so much as a protest.

The marriage had been a terrible mistake, and they both knew it. Alex hadn't trusted her enough, and because of his lack of trust the marriage had been split right down the middle.

He had been swayed by the spiteful lies of a spoilt and wilful youth—his own brother. Natasha knew she could never forgive him for that. Neither would she be able to forgive Roger.

Perhaps they would have survived it if it had all happened before their marriage. Perhaps there would have been enough room for them to sort it out. But it was all in the past now. Just the result of a tangled mess of people, hopeless marriage without trust, without faith, and there was no point in thinking of it now.

She eyed him wearily. 'Why don't you?' she said. 'Perhaps Roger will jump on the bandwagon and speak to the press too.'

Alex's mouth tightened. 'Don't speak about my brother like that,' he ordered in a tight voice. 'I don't blame him for what happened. He was only seventeen.'

Natasha gave him a bitter smile. 'Oh, he was very clever for seventeen, wasn't he?'

His eyes narrowed. 'What do you mean by that?' he demanded in a flat voice.

She shrugged slim shoulders, looking away from him. Her eyes focused on a painting on the wall, noting the different colours the artist had used.

'Well?' Alex was watching her intently.

She sighed, suddenly drained of all tension. 'He knew where to stick the knife in,' she said slowly, turning her head back, and wondering why they had to go through this again. 'He knew the best way to hurt me.'

There was a tense silence. 'Which was?' Alex asked slowly, his eyes narrowing.

Her eyes met his and she drew a deep breath. 'To hurt you enough to make you hate me,' She studied his face for a few moments, then shrugged again, recognising the look of disbelief on his features. She had known it would be pointless.

She moved away from him, and his hands dropped to his sides as he let her go. She moved over to the table, resting her hands on it and looking at nothing in particular.

'I knew you wouldn't believe me,' she said quietly into the silence.

Alex drew a ragged breath. 'What makes you think my brother should want to hurt either of us?'

She turned to look at him. Is it worth wasting my breath? she thought bitterly. Will he even hear my words?

She shrugged again and sighed. 'Roger was jealous of you. He wanted to be a big star, and he wanted to have your luck with women.' She frowned, thinking a little more on the subject. 'I suppose he also wanted to impress you.'

Alex watched her intently, his gaze speculative. 'What does any of that have to do with you?' he asked flatly. 'Unless you were helping to soothe his jealousy.'

Natasha tightened her lips, feeling a desire to hit out at him. How could he be so callous? 'Alex, it was never anything to do with me as a person!' she said angrily.

He tilted his head to one side, sliding both hands in his pockets and raising his brows. 'Of course not,' he said. 'We both know what the object of his affections was.'

Her fists clenched. 'He wanted me because I was yours and he couldn't have me!' she snapped between her teeth.

Temper flashed in his eyes, his nostrils flaring white as red colour flowed into his face. 'But you soon put a stop to that, didn't you, Natasha?' he said bitingly. 'You felt sorry for him and gave him what he wanted.'

She took a step towards him, her hands clenching at her sides.

'I gave him nothing!' she breathed in a low, angry voice.

His cruel black eyes fastened on her. 'You must think I'm stupid,' he bit out between teeth that were strong and white, 'to believe a cheating little bitch like you against my own flesh and blood!'

She struggled with her own temper for a brief moment, her eyes flashing, hating him for the way he treated her. The calm that had settled between them had gone, replaced by an explosive atmosphere, held together by bitterness and hatred. The air tingled with electricity as they watched each other, holding their own anger close to themselves.

Natasha felt tears sting her eyes at the hopelessness, the futility of it. There was nothing she could do, no words she could use to make him believe her. Theirs was a lost cause, a sinking ship in an oasis of pain and bitter, locked up memories.

'You are stupid, Alex,' she said bitterly, her eyes filled with tears of anger.

His hands gripped her shoulders. 'I've warned you before,' he said, his mouth biting out the words, 'don't speak to me like that.' He stared at her angrily.

'Open your eyes!' she cried, frustrated by her own helplessness as she saw the disbelieving anger on his face.

His gaze flicked over her with distaste. 'My eyes are open,' he said between his teeth, 'and what I see is a deceitful little trollop.' He pushed her away from him and slammed out of the door.

CHAPTER FOUR

NATASHA didn't hear from Alex for the next two days. She wasn't surprised, because after the terrible row they had had she didn't expect him to want to see her any more than was necessary. He had been bitterly angry, and she had seen the violence in his face, seen the taut control he had kept over his temper.

She knew it had been difficult for him to keep himself from behaving even more violently towards her, but she wasn't grateful to him for his self control. She felt unfairly treated. What had happened between them had been nothing to do with her. She had been a pawn in his and his brother's hands, and they had fought over her bitterly, throwing her out of their lives without even a thought as to why it had all happened in the first place. Some day, perhaps, she would be able to feel calm when she thought of it, but at the moment all she could feel was bitter anger towards Alex and his brother.

She had lunch with Marney two days after her argument with Alex because she was very worried about his statement about the sex scenes. Alex was quite capable of lying—but she had to make sure.

Marney was amused. 'Who told you that?' he asked with a smile as they sat in the shade of the beach restaurant opposite her hotel.

Natasha felt inwardly relieved; obviously Alex

had been lying to hurt her. 'Oh,' she said, flicking a napkin over her lip, 'no one in particular. I just heard a rumour and wanted to make sure there was no truth in it.'

Marney crumbled a roll between round fingers. 'Well, take it from me—you can forget you ever heard it.' He wagged his finger firmly at her. 'There are no sex scenes in this picture. It's supposed to be an exciting, romantic film about love and adventure.'

Natasha smiled. 'It was the adventure bit that was bothering me,' she said drily. 'Some directors do try to make films more commercial by putting more sex in them.'

Marney clucked his tongue. 'What do you think we are?' he asked, spreading his hands. 'A bunch of philistines? Why should we want to re-write a beautiful piece of literature and destroy its simplicity by putting lots of unwanted sex in it?'

Natasha frowned. 'I didn't know you'd read the book, Marney?' she said, surprised. Marney, as far as she knew, hadn't read a book in his life—with the possible exception of *Janet and John*, and then only through force.

'Well,' he blustered, 'I haven't exactly read it . . . but I do know the story.'

Natasha felt herself smile. They ate their lunch slowly, relaxing in the warm, heated atmosphere of the beach. Holidaymakers played noisily in the sea, the happy buzz of their laughter acting as a tonic. The lazy hum of a motorboat soothed the atmosphere as a waterskier tried his luck on the calm, golden-dappled sea.

'How are you getting on with Alex?' Marney asked suddenly, pouring himself some more wine.

Natasha looked away into the distance, her eyes gliding over the people on the beach. 'Oh, I haven't seen much of him, to tell you the truth,' she said.

He watched her shrewdly. 'Your choice—or his?'

She looked down at her hands with a little smile. 'A little of both, I think,' she said quietly. 'We only argue when we see each other, so it's a mutual decision not to talk if we don't have to.'

Marney nodded sagely. 'Good idea,' he said. 'I wouldn't want you to be too upset for filming.'

Natasha looked up with a wry expression, her eyes calm. 'Business comes first in all things, right?' she said, knowing that he was right to think that way—especially when the situation was as explosive as it was between her and Alex.

Marney's eyes were kind. 'No hard feelings, kid,' he said, 'but being hurt is better than being hurt and out of work. If you see what I mean.'

She did. He's right, she thought with a sigh. If Alex was going to make her pay for something she didn't do, she was better off staying in work, keeping herself busy, rather than being alone, having time to brood and lick her wounds.

'By the way,' Marney added casually, picking at a cheese straw, 'you never did tell me exactly what happened between you.' He looked up carefully, his eyes watchful.

'No,' said Natasha with a slow smile, 'I didn't, did I?' She eyed him in a silence that said more than words. They had an easy understanding between them, a rapport which told Marney now that he wasn't going to find out the truth until she decided to tell him.

He sighed ruefully, but there was respect in his gaze. 'Like trying to get blood out of a stone,' he muttered, grinning. 'Ah well, I guess I'll just have to go into the priesthood and hear your deathbed confession!'

Natasha laughed. He was probably right, because she doubted if she would ever feel up to telling anyone what had happened between them.

They ate the rest of their lunch, talking casually, laughing over stories Marney told her about the people he had been dealing with on the film set of *The Devil's Mistress*. He had obviously been very busy since she last saw him, even though that was only two or three days ago.

Marney left her after they finished lunch, and Natasha watched him go with a smile. He did his best to look after her, but somehow he always managed to make a mess of things. Still, he was a good agent, one of the best, and he had got her very good work all her career.

She stayed in the restaurant for a little while longer, sitting on her own, just thinking things over, trying to calm her mind. Then she left the beach, walking up the bleached stone steps to the main road above.

'Oh, my God!' she breathed in disbelief as she saw Alex leaning casually against a black sports car which glittered and shone in the hot sunlight.

She dived off in the opposite direction, hoping

he wouldn't notice her. But Alex saw her out of the corner of his eye and followed her. Natasha broke into a run, but Alex was quicker.

'Not so fast!' he bit out, his hand clamping down on her shoulder as he yanked her back easily. She landed against his chest with a thud that made her head spin.

He turned her round slowly. 'That's better,' he drawled, his mouth twisting, 'I'm getting sick of seeing the back of your head every time I try to talk to you.'

She looked up at him, shading her eyes from the sun. 'Why are you here, Alex?' she asked, keeping her voice controlled although inside she was angry at the way he manhandled her.

'I've just told you,' he said, 'I want to talk to you.'

Natasha eyed him warily. There was a stillness about him, a tension in the way he moved, the way he spoke. Something had happened to make him angry with her, but she didn't understand what it was.

'Go ahead,' she replied, spreading her hands with acceptance, glad that the crowds of people kept her safe from any threat of violence from him.

'Not here,' he said flatly, his eyes skimming the crowds before looking back at her. 'There are too many people. I'd prefer somewhere with more privacy.'

'Well, I wouldn't!' Natasha pointed out, studying him with a sense of unease. If he wanted more than a quick conversation, she would have bet her life that he was going to get angry with her again, and she wanted to avoid any repetition of their last argument.

His mouth tightened. 'That's too bad,' he said bluntly, taking her arm and leading her along the pavement. 'I don't have much time, and I'm not wasting what I do have arguing with you in the middle of the street.'

She walked slowly, dragging her feet. Then she saw the long black sports car, and her eyes widened with sudden realisation. She pulled back from him.

'Oh no,' she said firmly, 'I'm not getting in that car with you. You can't make me.'

Alex turned his head. 'Can't I?' he asked softly.

Something in his voice made her look at him sharply. His face held a grim determination, the sharp bones taking on a menacing look. But there were so many people around. It was a busy main street—surely he wouldn't pick her up and carry her in the car?

Alex leaned over and clicked open the car door, and the chrome flashed in the sunlight. 'Get in,' he said, watching her. Then: 'Don't make me lose my temper with you, Natasha.'

Their eyes warred briefly, then Natasha tightened her lips in defeat, her eyes a brilliant, angry blue. There was no arguing with him when he was in a mood like this. It was like trying to argue with a hungry tiger.

He strode quickly round to the other side as Natasha slid into the passenger seat. He started the car without a word and they shot away, driving along the coast.

'Where are we going?' she asked, looking at him

through her lashes. His profile was etched harshly in the glittering sun.

'To wait for telephone call,' he told her without bothering to go into further details.

Natasha smoothed down a fold in her bright cotton skirt, biting her lip. She was going to find out sooner or later, so why didn't he tell her now?

They drove on in silence for what seemed hours, but could only have been about thirty minutes. Then the car eased off the main mountain road and pulled into a private drive, leading up to a white, sunbleached villa which stood in a grove of olive-green trees and shrubbery.

Natasha felt her heart sink into her boots. The place was obviously deserted. There was a heavy silence that clung to the villa, making her more nervous and uneasy than before.

Alex got out of the car and came round to help her, his hand on hers as she stepped from the car. She looked up at the quiet, peaceful villa and wondered why they were here.

'Aren't you coming in?' Alex asked over his shoulder as he walked towards the door.

She sighed heavily, and followed, knowing that she had little choice. The big oak door swung open easily as Alex unlocked it and went into the cool hallway.

'Drink?' he asked, going into a spacious room to his left. Natasha followed him quietly, looking around.

'Will we be here long?' she asked, watching as he poured himself a whisky.

Alex looked over his shoulder, his face straight.

'That depends,' he answered briefly, putting the decanter back among the row of bottles in the wood-lined bar.

Natasha moistened her lips with her tongue, her sense of unease increasing. 'On what?'

He gave her a tight smile. 'On the contents of the phone call.' He eyed her. 'Do you want a drink or not?'

She nodded, her hands trailing over the luxurious feel of the thick leather armchair in the centre of the room. 'I'd like some Advocaat, if you have any,' she told him.

Alex gave her a smile. 'Very wise,' he said sardonically. 'Advocaat isn't likely to go to your head.' He went over to the cabinet again and took out a tall bottle with thick golden liquid in it. 'Lemonade?' he queried, capping the bottle again and reaching for another as Natasha nodded in agreement.

She looked round the room, taking in the luxurious furnishing, the cool, peaceful atmosphere of the room, which was gradually beginning to lose over to the tension inside her. Plants hung in little wicker baskets from the walls, surrounded by delicate summer furniture. The only concession to winter was the one solitary leather armchair.

'Whose villa is this?' she asked, walking to the open glass doors at one end of the room and looking out.

'It belongs to a friend of mine,' he said behind her. 'He lent it to me for a few months—it's easier than staying in a hotel. I get sick of hotel rooms.'

She looked round. 'Yes, they can get very lonely,' she agreed.

Alex handed her her drink, his long fingers brushing hers. 'Drink as much as you like,' he told her. 'You might want something stronger later.' His eyes watched her coolly.

She frowned. 'Why should I want something stronger?' she asked nervously.

His hard mouth twisted into a smile. 'I've told you already. Why must you be so impatient to hear bad news?' His eyes flicked over her. 'Surely you can wait just a little while longer before I satisfy your eager curiosity?'

Natasha bit her lip, her hands clinging to the smooth surface of the glass. 'Alex, stop talking to me in riddles! Tell me why you've brought me here.'

There was a little silence, then Alex turned and walked a few steps across the room. He took a drink of the whisky in his hand, as if weighing up his words before he spoke.

'Alex?' she queried, watching his lean body, the back of his black head.

He looked back at her as though he had forgotten she was there, then he raked a hand through his hair. 'Very well, if you must know.' He looked down at his glass, swirling the ginger liquid with one hand. 'I've heard disquieting rumours from England.'

She frowned, taking a step towards him. 'What about?'

'Us,' he said flatly, looking up at her. He saw the look in her eyes and nodded, 'Yes—they've found out about us too.'

Natasha caught her lower lip between her teeth.

Surely they already knew the press had been talking to someone? Or rather, she thought bitterly, that someone had been talking to the press.

'I have a reporter friend,' continued Alex, 'who tells me that Fleet Street is buzzing with the news. They haven't been able to confirm it yet, of course, but all they have to do is dig just a little bit deeper.'

'They know we had . . .' she stopped, unable to say it for a moment. Then she looked back at him, her eyes studying him earnestly. 'They know we had an affair?'

He gave her an ironic smile. 'I'm afraid it's a little more complex than that, my dear. If it hadn't been, I wouldn't have brought you here.' His eyes studied her assessingly, 'I want to find out if you know anything about it.'

Natasha caught at his arm as he turned away. 'About what? What's happened?'

Alex turned back to her, his gaze skimming over her coolly. 'Nothing,' he said bluntly, 'yet.' He moved closer to her. 'I hope for your sake that no one decides to publish any of the rumours, because if they do, I'll know who to blame, won't I?'

Realisation hit her, and her eyes widened in alarm. Someone had been spreading rumours in London that she had been married to Alex—still was married to Alex; and only one person could have done something like that. Roger.

She closed her eyes briefly on a groan of disbelief. If the news was confirmed and released, her life wouldn't be worth living. They would all know the details of her marriage, and Alex would make her life a perpetual hell.

Alex read her thoughts shrewdly. 'Yes,' he said flatly, 'they know we were married. They've got hold of the news from somewhere, Natasha.' He studied her in silence for a moment. 'I just hope it isn't from you.'

She opened her eyes on a flare of temper. 'Don't be so stupid!' she snapped angrily, her lips tightening. 'Why should I want to tell them? For all I know, it was you. You're more than capable of doing something like that to hurt me!'

His eyes narrowed, glinting like polished chips of jet. 'I have more effective ways of hurting you,' he drawled unpleasantly, 'or do you need to be reminded of them?'

Natasha watched him with hatred. Why did he have to keep trying to hurt her? She had never done anything to hurt him in her life. His brother had been the one to drive the nail between them. If Alex was fool enough to believe the spiteful lies of a jealous youth, then he deserved everything he got!

She eyed him bitterly. 'Oh, I don't need to be reminded,' she said between her teeth. 'I'm only too well aware of your methods. I'm surprised you don't beat old ladies up as well, I'm sure you'd enjoy it far more.'

His eyes flashed with temper. 'You acid-tongued little bitch!' he said bitingly, his hand reaching out to capture her arms, dragging her towards him.

The telephone shrilled into the silence, and Natasha breathed a heavy sigh of relief. Saved by the bell, she thought shakily as Alex let her go and strode over to the telephone table.

He picked up the ivory receiver. 'Yes?' he said curtly, his black head bent. He leant on the edge of the table, his long legs crossed as he listened.

Natasha shifted uneasily, trying to read the expression on his face, which was gradually darkening.

'If you print that Jack, I'll ...' he bit off his words as a burst of sound came from the earpiece. 'I don't give a damn who told you. No, I don't.' Then he paused, and his eyes raised to meet Natasha's, narrowing suddenly. 'Who *was* your source?' he asked slowly.

Natasha listened with her blonde head tilted to one side. Obviously, this was Alex's journalist friend. What Alex was saying didn't sound too favourable—no doubt they were going ahead with the story.

'I see,' Alex said tightly. 'Very well, if you're going to publish the damned thing, go ahead.' He listened for a moment, then said tightly, 'Yes, I know it's your job, but strictly off the record, I'll break your bloody neck if I ever set eyes on you again!' He slammed the receiver into place and stared at it broodingly.

'What is it?' Natasha asked, half aware of the news, half wishing he would tell her it was all a mistake.

He drank the rest of his whisky before replying. 'They're going ahead with the story,' he said flatly, standing up and walking over to the drinks cabinet.

'Oh ...' She couldn't think of anything to say,

her eyes widening as the full repercussions of the story hit her. They would be followed, hounded by the press for the next year at least—working together constantly, in each other's pockets while camermen crept up on them, reporters pushed questions at them. She wouldn't be able to take it. Alex wouldn't either—and she knew who he would turn on in his rage.

'Yes,' drawled Alex, pouring whisky into his glass, 'oh.'

She looked across at him, her eyes travelling over his broad back. 'What are we going to do?'

He turned, the dark brows lifting. 'You should have thought about that before you got in touch with Fleet Street.'

She blinked in disbelief. 'I don't understand . . .' she began, but he broke in with a barbed smile.

'Don't play the innocent with me, Natasha. You understand better than I do. What did you think would happen?' His voice was angry, sardonic. 'Did you think I'd break my contract and leave if you created enough trouble? Did you want me to leave you alone so desperately?'

Natasha frowned, shaking her head. 'I didn't. I didn't have anything to do with it.'

Alex looked down at his drink and slid one hand in his pocket. 'You must dislike me more than I thought,' he muttered roughly, then looked up again, his gaze meeting hers. He took three strides towards her to stand close to her, his gaze brooding. 'Is that it, Natasha? Do you hate me so much that you'd tell the world about our marriage?'

She shook her head in disbelief, her frown

deepening. He blamed her at every turn. 'Why should I do that? I'm the one who'll come out of this the worst, not you.'

There was a little silence, then he said, 'It makes very little difference now.' He raked a hand through his hair. 'They've had direct confirmation, and they can print what the hell they like. I should count myself lucky they bothered to warn me beforehand.'

Natasha wondered why they had. Perhaps they had been dubious as to whether the story was true. After all, she had to admit it sounded more like a publicity stunt than fact. What could be more exciting than knowing that the two leading players in a film had once been married, and come through a stormy separation? It would create no end of trouble and interest for them.

'Alex,' she said quietly into the silence, 'you have to believe me, I didn't talk to the press.'

'Damn you!' He put his glass down with a crash, his face angry. 'Don't lie to me!'

She backed slightly, shaking her head. 'I'm not! Please believe me . . .'

'Believe you?' he asked through his teeth. 'Why should I believe you? Ever since we met you've told me nothing but a string of lies. What makes you think I'd believe you now?'

'That isn't true,' she said through dry lips. 'I've never lied to you.'

His hands came down on her shoulders, clamping hard on her skin as he dragged her towards him. 'My God,' he muttered angrily, 'what do you take me for? Do you think you can convince me with those big blue eyes of yours? One look at them and any man's sunk—but not me,' he said grimly, 'not any more. You've tried it on once too often.'

Her temper flared, her eyes blazing angrily. 'Don't be so stupid!' she snapped between her teeth. 'Can't you see what's in front of your own nose? You're blind as well as stupid!'

'Oh no, Natasha,' he gritted, 'not blind. I can recognise guilt when I see it, and I saw it when Roger came in behind me that night . . . I only had to take one look at your face to see he was telling the truth.'

She tried to twist out of his grasp, wrench herself free, but he was too strong for her and her efforts were futile. 'It wasn't true!' she told him in a low angry voice. 'He was lying.'

Alex shook his head. 'I saw your face, your eyes . . . the way you looked at him . . .' His face darkened with the memories. 'I'm not a fool, Natasha. I know what I saw.'

It was hopeless. He would never believe her. She gave up trying to convince him, and began to struggle against the iron hold of his arms, pushing her fists against his chest. But he held her still, his arms tightening their hold on her until she crushed hard against him, her face creased with pain.

'Let me go!' she shouted, trying to pull away again.

He ignored her, his hand biting into her wrists as his other hand shot out to push into her back, dragging her back against him with a thud. Natasha swayed, her legs unsteady, her breathing erratic, while Alex slipped his other arm around her to hold her pinioned, imprisoned against him by the steel bands of his arms.

'You're hurting me!'

His lips curled into a taunting smile. 'Good. I enjoy hurting you—it makes me feel better.'

Her eyes widened in her flushed face. 'You swine!' she hissed, unable to believe her own ears. How could he be so callous, so totally unforgiving?

Alex ignored that. 'Why did you do it, Natasha? They told me who'd confirmed it. You knew they wouldn't print it unless they had direct confirmation from either one of us. No one else knows, after all.'

'Your brother knew!' she said angrily, her eyes sparking a fiery blue.

'My brother,' he bit out, 'doesn't sound like you on the telephone or hadn't that occurred to you?' He noticed her stricken look, her eyes wide in her flushed face. 'Oh yes, they told me who their source was.'

'But . . .' She was lost for words, incredulous. How could it have happened? They must have got it wrong, she thought wildly, it must have been a mistake. 'I didn't ring them, Alex,' she said desperately. 'I was out nearly all day.'

His mouth twisted into a harsh bitter smile. 'I don't believe you, my dear. You'll have to try better than that.'

'What do you want from me? An alibi?' she asked angrily.

His eyes fell on her mouth, his breathing quickening. 'No,' he said in a slow, thickening voice, 'something much more interesting than that.'

Too late she realised what he meant to do. She shook her head, her hands beginning to tremble, and tried to pull away. He was stronger, his hands taking her shoulders and pulling her back harshly. His hand caught at her blouse, making one of the buttons fly off.

'Stop fighting me,' he muttered against her lips, then his eyes fell on her now bare breast, watching the soft white flesh as it heaved with the force of her emotions.

'Don't ...' she whispered in breathless panic, feeling her heart thud with a crazy rhythm, her legs weakening until she couldn't move them if she had tried.

Alex stared at her breast for a moment, then slowly he reached out a hand and ripped the rest of her blouse away, leaving her naked to the waist.

'My God ...' he muttered thickly, 'you're beautiful!' and his hands reached out to cup her breasts, making her shiver with fear and excitement, a groan escaping from her mouth as he stroked her nipples with long fingers.

His mouth clamped over hers, heated, sensual, coaxing, his hands moving over her naked skin with a slow heated sensuality, making her shudder against him in mass confusion. His hands slid under her knees and he scooped her up in his arms, carrying her out of the living room and into a bedroom on the other side of the hall. Natasha watched in anguish as the bed came closer and closer, filling her with fear.

Then her mind woke up, and her legs started to

work. 'No!' she screamed, jumping out of his arms
and running for the door. But Alex caught her and
whirled her round, his face savage, and pushed her
roughly on to the bed. She landed with a thud, her
head sinking into the soft pillows.

Her heart thudded hard as she watched him
unbutton his shirt with fingers that trembled. His
face was filled with dark colour, his eyes passionate.

Natasha swallowed as he knelt on the bed beside
her. 'Don't do this, Alex,' she whispered, tears
stinging the back of her eyes.

'Lie down!' he bit out, pushing her back against
the pillows with one long hand as she tried to sit
up.

His mouth took hers, roughly at first, then the
kiss changed to a sweet exquisite pleasure, his lips
coaxing as his hands slid hungrily over her naked
skin. His hand was on her thigh and she tried to
push him away with one trembling hand.

'No . . .' she pleaded through aching lips, her
eyes wide and startled.

He slowly raised his black head, his black eyes
glinting into hers. 'Yes,' he said thickly, and his
tongue snaked out across her mouth, making her
catch her breath with excitement.

Her breasts swelled in his experienced hands and
he groaned, his mouth closing over her darkening
nipples. His hands wrung a bitter, frantic response
from her, until they twisted together on the bed in
spiralling excitement.

They were interrupted by the sound of the telephone, shrilling into the silence of their breathing.

Alex raised his head, listening intently, waiting for the ringing to stop. But it just went on.

'Hell!' he muttered, pushing himself off her and rolling to the other side of the bed to pick up the phone. 'Yes?' he said in a clipped voice as he picked up the receiver.

Natasha didn't dare move. She closed her eyes in a silent prayer of thanks to whoever had decided to ring at that precise moment. That was the second time her neck had been saved at the last moment.

Alex swore under his breath. 'Are you sure?' he asked, his black head bent as he listened. Then he nodded. 'Right, thanks for letting me know.' He put the phone down and turned back to her.

Natasha shrank away from him, scared that he would start making love to her again, but Alex flicked cold eyes over her. 'You needn't worry. We haven't got time,' he said abruptly, then stood up, picking his shirt up and slipping into it. 'You'd better get dressed,' he told her, his eyes falling on her half naked body.

She moved limply, her eyes not moving from him. 'Who was it?' she asked as she fumbled with the few remaining buttons on her blouse.

He tucked his shirt into the waistband of his black trousers, and buttoned up the cuffs. 'A friend of mine in Nice,' he told her in an impersonal voice. 'He advised me to leave here immediately.'

Natasha frowned, holding her blouse together at the top with still hands. She tilted her head to one side. 'Why?'

Alex eyed her. 'The *paparazzi* are apparently on their way over.'

At that instant, a light flashed from the open window behind them, and all they could see was a swarthy grinning face behind a camera, before Alex leapt at the window, his face murderous.

CHAPTER FIVE

NATASHA scampered into the living room, her hands over her face. Now Alex would be even more furious, but at least this time he couldn't blame her. She hadn't been out of his sight for a second since they had arrived at the villa, so he couldn't say she had rung the press and told them where to find them.

As she sat down in the living room, she saw some faces outside the large glass doors, and leapt up again, turning her face while the flashbulbs popped furiously. Oh no! she thought, hurrying off and trying to find a room which was not plagued by grinning faces and cameras. The kitchen appeared to be safe, the window shielded by a rather strange assortment of plants which hung like bindweed from the ceiling to the floor.

She busied herself by peering in cupboards while she waited for Alex to return. The kitchen was rather small, however, and she soon ran out of cupboards. She wondered whether she was supposed to sit there for ever, waiting for him. I could always make myself some coffee, she mused, biting her lip as she tried to remember which cupboard had had the coffee jar in it.

She hummed to herself as she spooned coffee in a large French bowl and waited for the kettle to boil on the electric hob in the corner, then heard a sound behind her.

Alex lounged in the doorway, his white shirt stained with mud. 'What,' he asked irritably, 'do you think you're doing?'

She gnawed her lower lip, looking guiltily at the coffee cup. 'I didn't think you'd mind,' she said nervously, then gave him what passed for a bright smile. 'Did you want some?'

His face looked murderous for a split second, then he sighed, raking a hand through his hair. 'I might as well,' he shrugged, looking over his shoulder towards the front door. 'We're not likely to get out of here for a while.'

Natasha took another coffee bowl out of the cupboard and spooned coffee in it. 'How did they know we were here?' she asked quietly

He shrugged. 'Word gets around. Everybody seemed to know where I was staying, and as soon as the news got out that we'd been married, they all piled over here.'

Natasha felt her fists clench at the thought of everyone reading about her marriage. Her mind flashed a picture of that cameraman's grinning leer as he took the picture in the bedroom, and felt sick to her stomach. She looked back at Alex through her lashes.

'Did you get the film?' she asked.

He frowned as though he'd forgotten, then sighed. 'Oh, no.' He grimaced, looking down at his shirt, indicating the muddy stains. 'I tripped over.'

Natasha nodded, then reached over to pick up the kettle as it boiled, and poured the water into their cups.

'Thanks,' said Alex as he took the coffee from her and laid it on one of the surfaces. 'I couldn't spot him among the crowd because they all looked so much alike.' He shrugged. 'I could hardly attack each one of them and smash their cameras up— much as I'd like to!'

Natasha looked down at the floor, feeling her cheeks flush hotly. 'Do you think they'll use it?' she asked huskily, knowing that if the picture came out properly it would be highly incriminating for both of them. She shuddered at the thought of it on the front pages.

He lifted dark brows sardonically. 'What do you think? Of course they'll use the damned thing. I bet they couldn't believe their luck when they arrived to find you here!'

She felt herself flush under his steady gaze. 'You shouldn't have brought me,' she said, almost to herself.

Alex gave a harsh laugh. 'What was I supposed to do?' he queried, 'argue on the beach with you where everyone could see for themselves? They wouldn't have needed a camera then, would they?'

Natasha turned accusing eyes on him. 'You know that wasn't what I meant!' she said in a low, angry voice. 'If you weren't such a swine none of this would ever have happened!'

His eyes flashed angrily in return and he put his cup down, raising his brows at her. 'Me? I like that! Let me remind you that if you hadn't rung the bloody animals in the first place, we wouldn't be in this mess.'

She controlled her temper, biting back a retort

and turned away from him. She hadn't meant that and he knew it. He was just evading the issue because he knew he had had no right to force her into his bed. He had done it quite simply because at the time he had wanted her, and when Alex Brent wanted something, he stopped at nothing to get it. She knew him of old.

She drank her coffee, tasting the bitter thick liquid slide down her throat, calming her a little by the sting of its heat.

Alex stood up. 'There's no point in staying here,' he said abruptly. 'Come on, we might as well battle through. I'll drive you back to the Negresco.'

She looked down at herself in consternation and grabbed at his arm as he turned to walk out of the little kitchen. 'I can't go like this!' she told him.

He eyed the bare expanse of flesh and frowned, his eyes resting on the torn blouse and missing buttons. 'I see your point,' he agreed, fingering the light cotton as he tried to pull the two halves of the blouse together. 'No use,' he said, giving up. 'Wait here and I'll bring you one of mine.'

Natasha closed her eyes on a groan of disbelief, but he had already vanished. She could hardly wear one of his shirts—it would only look more obvious if she went out wearing nothing at all.

Alex returned and handed her a white silk shirt. 'It'll be a bit hot in that, so I should roll the sleeves up.'

She took the shirt. 'Alex,' she said patiently, 'I can't wear this. They'll know I've left my own clothes in here, and they'll have the time of their lives thinking up good reasons why.'

He raised one brow. 'Would you rather be photographed in that?' he asked, pointing to the torn blouse she wore.

Natasha had to agree with him; his shirt was by far the better idea. She began to unbutton it, then looked quickly at him. 'Would you turn round?' she asked worriedly.

His eyes widened slowly with surprise. 'Don't be absurd! I've seen you with less on, remember?'

She flushed. 'Please,' she asked in a quiet voice, and it worked. Alex sighed and turned round, his back to her. Natasha hastily stripped the torn blouse off and slipped into his, rolling the sleeves up and tucking it in to make it look less conspicuous.

'You can turn around now,' she told him at last, and he turned, raising his dark brows.

'Not bad,' he commented, then began to walk out into the cool hallway. 'Ready?' he asked as they reached the door, and Natasha nodded, feeling rather nervous.

The cameras clicked furiously as they made their way to the car, ignoring the reporters' hurried, frantic questions in French. Alex's face was stony as he started the car and they shot away out of the drive and on to the main road.

'Serve them right if I ran one of them over!' he muttered under his breath as they narrowly missed a photographer who shook his fist at them.

They drove quickly along the Corniche road until at last they came back down into Nice and cruised along the sea-front. The hotel was plagued with reporters, scurrying around outside the main entrance while the doorman stood watching imperviously.

'They're like fleas,' Alex muttered angrily, turning the car round to drive to the back entrance, 'they multiply the minute you take your eyes off them!'

Natasha looked out of the window surreptitiously, trying not to be recognised. The back entrance, fortunately, was clear, and Alex pulled up in front of it.

'Go straight in,' he told her, leaning over and clicking on the door, 'and don't talk to them.'

She looked back at him as she got out of the car. 'Is there anything you can do to stop them printing that picture?' she asked softly, her eyes scanning his face for a sign of hope.

'No,' he said flatly, leaning over to close the door. 'You brought this on yourself—don't ask me to get you out of it.' He gave her one last angry look, then pressed hard on the accelerator and sped away, leaving Natasha to watch the car disappear down the narrow street.

She went up to her room with stealth, ignoring the avid glances of the people who recognised her on the way. At least she had avoided the French newspapermen, she mused as she got to her room and closed the door behind her with a sigh of relief.

The telephone started ringing the minute she walked in, but she ignored it, making a face at it and going into the bathroom. She felt so hot and tired that what she wanted most was a long hot bath. She selected a soft, perfumed bubble bath from her stock in the cupboard and poured it into the large tub.

While the water was running she went into the bedroom again and picked up some clothes to wear. The telephone began ringing again, but she took great pleasure in ignoring it. Now where did I put that book? she thought, frowning, and hunted all over the bedroom before she found it tucked away in a drawer.

Typical, she thought, taking it into the bathroom. She was always putting her things in safe places, but they were so safe she could never remember where they were!

She savoured the long, hot bath, relaxing her aching muscles in the perfumed water. She read part of the book, topping up the water every time it started to lose heat. By the time she got to chapter eight, she was almost asleep, and decided it was time to get out and get dressed.

It was while she was dressing that she started wondering why Roger had told the press she was married to Alex. What did he possibly have to gain? Her frown deepened and she did the buttons up slowly on her white cotton dress.

Alex had said it was she who had telephoned them. So it had to be a woman. Roger's girl-friend? It's possible, she thought, frowning. But even if that was what had happened, it still didn't tell her anything about Roger's motive.

When she finally decided to answer the phone, it was Marney, in a state of consternation, bubbling over with incredulity.

'Is it true?' he babbled. 'Is it true?'

Natasha smiled to herself as she bent her golden head to the receiver. 'Yes, Marney, it's true.' She sat down on the bed. 'I'm sorry I didn't tell you before, but I just didn't feel up to talking about it.'

'You didn't, huh? Well, let me tell you something, my little Edwardian Princess, it's the best piece of publicity work you've ever done for me! I'll remind you about it next time you tell me you don't like the publicity depot.'

Natasha frowned, her eyes narrowing. 'What do you mean—I've done for you?' Suspicions formed in her mind.

'Well,' Marney explained, 'you rang them, didn't you?'

Her lips tightened. 'No, I didn't! Who told you that?'

'Well, nobody, but it says so right here in the paper.'

She closed her eyes, wondering if this nightmare would ever end. 'Which paper?'

She could almost hear Marney shrug. 'The *Standard*. I had a copy flown over to me right after lunch. I wasn't going to hang around to hear it from someone else—I wanted to read it for myself.' There was a distinct note of pride in his voice which made Natasha grit her teeth.

'Marney,' she said patiently, 'I did not ring them. I didn't know anything about it until Alex told me this afternoon.'

Marney chuckled. 'Alex?' he echoed, laughing. 'Oh dear, I still can't get over it! Is he really your husband? I always knew something pretty desperate must have happened between you two for him to scare you the way he did, but I never dreamed . . .'

Natasha listened to his flow of words, wondering if the whole world had gone mad, or if it was just her. The paper had obviously printed the news, together with their source. Clever, she thought, biting her lip. Now they couldn't deny it, seeing that it had supposedly come from her own lips.

'Are you still there?' Marney's voice crackled over the line and she looked back dumbly at the receiver in her hand.

'Yes, I'm still here.' She sighed heavily, shaking her head. 'But please believe me—I had nothing to do with that story.'

There was a little silence, then Marney said slowly, 'Really? It says here that you did, but then I guess you should know . . .'

She raised her eyes heavenwards. 'Marney, have I ever lied to you before?'

'Well, no . . .'

'Then you must know I'm not lying now. Besides,' she twirled the cord around her little finger, 'why should I ring them if I didn't even want you to know?'

'Mmm,' Marney agreed thoughtfully. There was another silence, then he said in a more serious tone, 'Have you any idea who might have done it? Alex maybe?'

She shook her head, her face grim. 'No, it wasn't him. But I have a pretty shrewd idea who did it. Don't let it worry you, though, I'll let you know if I find anything useful on that subject.'

Marney rang off and Natasha sat alone in her

hotel room, thinking of Roger. His anger towards her had been eaten up long ago; he should feel no more towards her. He had had his revenge.

Roger had wanted her badly when she was married and living with Alex. He had flirted with her every time his brother was out of sight, his eyes following her constantly whenever Alex was around. Natasha had felt uneasy with him at first, but had soon grown to feel rather sorry for him.

His jealousy of Alex had been understandable. Alex was a success, a famous film star whose rugged good looks had attracted women of all ages. He was rich, good-looking and famous, and Roger had thought he had everything he could possibly want. Then he had married Natasha, and Roger had realised that Alex's life was filled to the brim with everything that Roger himself wanted.

Then Alex had gone to Italy to make a brief appearance in a film, and Roger had taken his chance while he was away. He came after Natasha with everything her had, but she pushed him away, gently at first, trying not to hurt his feelings, aware that he was already bitterly envious of his brother.

After a fortnight of rejection, Roger turned nasty. He had tried to rape her one night after he had spent the evening watching her over the rim of a constantly refilled whisky glass.

Natasha had tried to stop him drinking early in the evening. 'I'm going to make some coffee,' she had said brightly, watching him through her lashes as he drank more of his brother's whisky. 'Wouldn't you like some?'

Roger had looked at her with glinting eyes. 'I'm

not stupid,' he had said with an angry mutter. 'You're trying to stop me drinking my precious brother's whisky, aren't you?'

She had bitten her lip worriedly. 'Don't you think you've had enough?' Her eyes had followed the flood of ginger liquid into his glass.

Roger had slammed the bottle down on the table, his face colouring with anger. 'I suppose you think I'm too young? Well, I'm not! I'm old enough to drink and I'm old enough for women!' He had stood up, swaying slightly, and grabbed for her.

Natasha had jumped away, her face showing her confusion. He was her brother-in-law and he was only seventeen. She hadn't known how to handle the situation.

'Please don't get upset, Roger,' she had said hastily, moistening her lips with her tongue.

Roger's drink-clouded eyes had followed the movement hungrily, his eyes squinting a little. 'That's nice,' he had said, his voice slurring. 'Do it again.'

She had swallowed, her hands twisting together, wishing Alex was here to deal with it. 'I think you'd better go to bed, Roger,' she had said quietly, her eyes sad.

He had grinned, his smooth young face breaking into a leer. 'What a good idea!' he had drawled in a poor imitation of Alex's voice. 'Why don't we go together?' His hand had reached out, grabbing her breast, and she moved backwards, her face crimson with embarrassment and anger.

'Go to bed, Roger!' she had told him angrily.

But Roger's lips had curled back in a sneer. 'Alone? What's the point in that?' He had given her a drunken grin. 'I'll bet you're dying for it by now. How long has he been gone—two and a half weeks?'

Her lips had tightened with anger. 'Don't speak like that!'

But he had ignored her, leaning forward, his finger wagging lecherously. 'Poor old Natasha, locked in your lonely room.' He stepped closer to her, and she backed until her back pressed against the wall. Roger grinned again. 'Why don't we go up to your room? He'll never know unless we tell him.'

She had tried to push past him, but Roger was strong for his age, and pushed her back harshly. 'Naughty!' he said, his face hardening. 'Mustn't try to run away from Roger.'

Natasha pressed hard against the wall, staring at him with wide eyes. 'Stop this, Roger,' she had said in what she hoped passed for a calm voice. 'Alex will kill you if you touch me.'

That was the wrong thing to say, because Roger's face tightened in jealous rage, his eyes squinting. 'I'm sick of his name, do you hear me? Don't say it again! Everyone thinks he's so bloody fantastic, but he's not. I'm just as good as him.' His voice had slurred. 'Look, I'll show you. I'm younger than he is!'

He had pressed his wet lips against hers in a disgusting mockery of a kiss. Natasha had squirmed in disgust, her hands beating at his while he touched her, pulling harshly at her as he tried to make love to her.

'Let me go!' she had snapped with angry, frightened contempt, pushing his face away with both hands.

Roger had been furious, swaying, his face filled with rage while she stared at him, breathing hard. Then he had lunged at her, ripping her dress while she ran for the door, kicking him away and running upstairs to her room.

Roger followed, but his movements were slurred by drink. She locked the door and stayed in her room, shivering while Roger swore and smashed things outside her room. Finally he had lurched into his own bedroom, leaving her alone to go through an agony of confusion.

She had avoided him like the plague for the next week. But in her mind she was torn apart, unsure as to whether she should tell Alex of his brother's behaviour. How could she possibly live in the same house with Roger after what had happened?

But the matter was taken out of her hands. Roger took her dressing gown and some of her clothes and slipped them into his room. He took some of his own clothes and hid them at the back of her wardrobe, and when Alex came home he displayed them as evidence. Alex had been torn apart, his face showing the agony of betrayal.

When Roger had confronted Natasha in front of Alex, her face had gone white with the shock, and the memory of that evening had come back to her, making her flush deeply, stammering out her innocence, trying to explain to Alex.

But her face had convinced him. He had taken her humiliation to be a sign of guilt. Natasha had

had a bitter argument with him, but it made no difference.

She had left the house the next day, numb, aching with bitterness. She had poured all her energies into her career, and had never looked back since. Until now . . .

Natasha spent the next three days hiding from the press and from the people she knew. She didn't want to have to spend hours making up excuses to her friends. Things were difficult enough as they were, without having extra loads to bear.

On Friday she flew to Paris to have a last fitting for her costumes in the film. The dressmaker, a flighty, nervous-looking Frenchwoman, oohed and aahed as she tried each one on.

'Oh, *chérie*,' she exclaimed, throwing her hands up in the air, her enormous collection of bracelets jangling, 'it is *magnifique!*'

Natasha looked down at the long off-the-shoulder crimson gown. 'Don't you think it's a little bright for my colouring?' she asked drily.

'*Non!*' cried the dressmaker, pursing her lips and shaking her black curls. 'You look *ravissante*! I have created a masterpiece. Every woman in the world will cry out with envy when they see you.'

Natasha doubted that, but she gave the woman a little smile and slipped the dress off. Paulette patted the silk folds lovingly.

'Now,' she said when they were finished, 'I think it is time we had something to eat. But first we ring some friends of mine and have them come along with us.'

Natasha protested. 'I'm not hungry, Paulette,' she said, hastily doing up the zip of her dress. 'I'd much rather go for a little walk around the city while I'm here.'

Paulette's birdlike hands flew to her face in horror. 'Not hungry? *Mon Dieu*, you are in Paris and you refuse to eat?' She shook her black curls. 'When you are in Paris, you eat well, like the French.' She went over to the telephone and dialled a number.

Natasha listened, straining her ears as she tried to make out the sound of rapid, gunfire French coming from Paulette's tiny red mouth. It was hopeless—the Parisians spoke like machineguns. She could never understand them.

'It is settled,' Paulette told her, going over to her desk and picking up her jacket. 'We meet at Maxim's.' She looked the picture of French chic, as though she had just stepped out of one of Coco Chanel's fitting rooms.

Natasha's eyes widened. 'Maxim's?' she queried, and smiled drily at the woman. 'Who's paying?'

Paulette threw up her hands in disgust. 'Money!' she exclaimed, walking briskly out of the office on slim birdlike legs. 'Always you think of money. Well, for your information, I tell you. Monsieur Jackson—he is paying.'

They drove to the restaurant in Paulette's zippy little Renault 5, darting in and out of the traffic at such speed that Natasha clung to the seat and prayed.

Paulette dodged off the Place de la Concorde and nipped in behind a Rolls-Royce along the kerb outside Maxim's. She handed her keys to the doorman outside the restaurant, giving him a quick look and a raise of her brows.

'Attend to this, *monsieur*,' she ordered, and floated past him.

Maxim's was exactly how Natasha had remembered it—the misted windows with 'Maxim's' engraved on them surrounded by oak panelling and heavy curtains, dark red carpeting and hosts of black-tie-and-tailed waiters. Their party was already there, seated in a corner in the first part of the restaurant, at a table for six.

A bottle of Maxim's champagne stood on the heavy damask tablecloth, and Natasha went over and sat down.

'Good to see you again, Natasha,' said B.B. Jackson, winking at her with little piggy eyes. 'Or should I call you Mrs Brent!' He guffawed, his large stomach heaving.

Oh dear, thought Natasha, this is the sort of lunch, it's going to be. She managed to parry their questions as she ate her lunch, starting with a bowl of delicious *crudités*. The man opposite her seemed to be a starving Frenchman and wolfed an entire steak in the time it took Natasha to eat one solitary potato.

Natasha was glad to escape after lunch. She told Paulette not to drive her back to her hotel.

'I'm quite capable of finding a taxi, Paulette,' she argued with her outside the restaurant.

'Pah!' exclaimed Paulette, wrinkling her tiny nose. 'You do not know our taxi drivers. They are pigs—absolute pigs!' She shook her hands, the bracelets crashing together. 'But you are determined. I will go home safely and leave you to your fate.'

She jumped into the car and sped off, leaving Natasha smiling after her on the pavement. The door of the restaurant behind her opened, and she turned her head on a reflex gesture.

'Roger!' she whispered, her face whitening as she watched Roger Brent walk out of the door.

CHAPTER SIX

ROGER had changed, his face no longer holding that bitter regret. He was taller, his height reminding her instantly of Alex as he walked towards her. His dark brown hair flopped over his eyes in the breeze and he pushed it back with a smooth hand, his brown eyes studying her worriedly.

'Hallo, Natasha,' he said quietly.

She looked away from him, her eyes dazed. 'Hallo,' she managed to say, a thousand questions running through her mind. He was in France—she hadn't expected that. She had expected him either to stay in London or fly to Nice—after all, he was the one who had created all the trouble.

'What are you doing here?' she asked, avoiding his eyes. She still couldn't bring herself to look at him; there were too many memories in that smooth face.

He shrugged. 'Nothing much.' His eyes squinted against the sun. 'I thought I'd take a holiday. I haven't been to Paris for ages, and I miss it sometimes.'

She nodded, looking down at the pavement. 'Well,' she said slowly, 'I really must be going now. I have some shopping to do and I have a flight to catch first thing in the morning.'

'No, don't go.' He caught at her arm. Natasha turned her head, studying him, and he shrugged self-deprecatingly, smiling a little as he looked at her. 'I want to talk to you.'

Her face hardened and she looked pointedly at her arm, and Roger's hand dropped away and fell to his side. He slid his hands in his pockets and rocked back and forth slightly on his heels.

A taxi passed at that moment and Natasha stuck her arm out, waving frantically. She walked towards it as it screamed to a halt and leant over to the driver's window.

'Place du Tertre, *s'il vous plaît*,' she said quickly to the driver, and he nodded.

She got into the taxi and glanced out of the window. Roger was standing where she had left him, his head bent as he watched her broodingly. Natasha suddenly felt sorry for him—he looked so lost standing on his own. But then her mind flashed a memory back and she tightened her lips, turning her head away. The taxi pulled away, and she sat in the back wondering why Roger was in France.

To cause more trouble? She frowned. He had caused quite enough for one lifetime; surely he didn't want to make her life even more painful than it was already?

She pushed Roger out of her mind and relaxed in the car as they sped towards Montmartre. It had been a long time since she had been to the Sacré Coeur. She wasn't going to let Roger's appearance spoil her trip more than it had already.

She arrived back in Nice the next day. The flight had tired her out—flying always did, no matter how long the distance to be covered. It was sitting

around at airports and sitting on planes that made
her tired, not getting from one place to another.

She went to her hotel straight away and took a
long hot bath before getting changed. She had to
have lunch with Cara at one, which meant she
would have to hurry down to meet her. She dressed
simply in white trousers and a black and gold
waistcoat. It was warm enough not to wear a
blouse under the waistcoat, and she was pleased
with her appearance. She looked rather smart.

She arrived downstairs on time and waited in
the foyer for Cara, sitting on a square seat in the
centre of the marble hall, relaxing as she watched
people coming in and out of the hotel.

Cara swept in looking elegant and sophisticated.
'Sorry I'm late, darling,' she said, grinning pleas-
edly as people stared at her in awe and recognition.
'Judd wouldn't drive me, so I had to get a taxi.'

Natasha smiled, standing up. 'Was he busy?'
Judd usually ran at Cara's beck and call; it was
most unusual for him to refuse to drive her.

Cara sighed as they walked through to La
Ronde, the hotel restaurant. 'Well, he had a million
things to do this afternoon. I tried to persuade him
to come along, but he was in one of his manly
moods, and gave a rather exciting display of mas-
culinity.' Her lips curled with the memory.

Lunch was served quickly, and they talked about
the coming production. The restaurant, La Ronde,
was a charming place with a circular design. A circular table was set in the centre of the room, with
leather stools round it, and an outer circle of tables
and chairs for more intimate relaxed meals sur-

rounded it. Toulouse-Lautrec nightclub posters
hung on the rich brown walls, and the atmosphere
was gay and lighthearted.

'How are you getting on with your leading man?'
asked Cara as she spooned the rich coffee ice cream
into her mouth. 'I hear he's quite a wow with his
leading ladies.'

Natasha frowned, looking up. That didn't sound
like the Alex she had married. He was certainly
very potent sexually, but he didn't generally sleep
with every woman he came across.

'To tell the truth,' she replied casually, 'I haven't
seen much of him since the celebration dinner.'

Cara raised a brow, running one hand across the
smooth top of her head, her chestnut brown hair
pulled back from her face. 'A friend told me he
usually makes a play for his co-stars—but my
friend could be wrong.' She looked down at her ice
cream and made a face. 'Get thee behind me,
Satan,' she said, pushing the plate away and lighting a cigarette. 'I'll get fat,' she told Natasha with
a smile.

Natasha smiled back, but felt heavy-hearted.
What Cara had said made her think of Alex when
she had wanted to forget him. Seeing Roger yesterday had made everything so much more vivid.
She just wanted to be able to put it all behind her.

'I won't be a minute,' said Cara, standing up, 'I
just want to go and powder my nose.' She winked
at Natasha and swayed away elegantly.

Natasha finished her coffee and waited for Cara
to return. She wondered whether Roger had just
been in Paris for a holiday, or whether the reasons

for his visit were more sinister. She hoped he
wouldn't come to Nice. She shuddered. Alex would
kill him if he came anywhere near her.

A movement in front of her made her look up.
'Alex!' she exclaimed, startled, as she looked into a
pair of malevolent black eyes.

'You don't mind if I join you for a moment, do
you?' he said curtly, sitting down on the chair
opposite her and resting his hands on the table.

Natasha looked around in consternation for
Cara. How had Alex suddenly appeared? He must
have been in the restaurant all along. Why didn't I
notice him? she thought irritably.

Alex read her mind easily. 'I was sitting over
there,' he said, pointing to a table across the room.
'If you'd been sitting where Cara was you would
have seen me.'

Natasha dropped her gaze from his. No doubt
Cara had seen him, and decided it wasn't worth
mentioning. Her mouth tightened, but she didn't
blame the other woman. How was she to know?

'You were in Paris yesterday, weren't you?' Alex
asked, studying her through hooded lids.

She looked up sharply. Had he seen her with
Roger? 'Yes,' she said slowly, 'I went to see
Paulette, for a costume fitting.'

Alex gave her a barbed smile. 'So did I,' he
drawled unpleasantly. 'Only I was there in the
afternoon.' He picked up a spoon and ran his long
fingers over it with chilling slowness. 'I drove past
Maxim's at about three.'

Natasha's heart stopped momentarily. She
closed her eyes for a second, trying to think. It had

been stupid of Roger to approach her in the street. She had known what would happen.

'Paulette took me to lunch,' she said with a slight stammer, avoiding his eyes as best she could.

There was a silence, then: 'I suppose you just bumped into Roger in the street, hmm? Is that what you'd like me to believe?' His tone was an insolent drawl.

She looked up, her face angry. 'That's exactly what happened,' she said, her hands lacing together tightly.

'And pigs fly,' snapped Alex, his mouth hardening. 'I drove past at the wrong time, it seems. You were just getting ready to kiss—it made a touching if rather incestuous picture.'

The insult took her breath away, and she leaned forward, her eyes sparking angrily. 'I did not kiss him!' she said between her teeth. 'I got straight into a taxi and went to Montmartre. I didn't even speak to him.'

His hand shot out and gripped her wrist as she tried to stand up. 'You're lying,' he said tightly, pulling her back into her chair. 'I've got eyes in my head. You were holding hands in the middle of the street and looking into each other's eyes.'

Natasha felt her hands tremble with anger. 'I'm not going to discuss it with you, Alex,' she said, keeping her voice low. 'It's none of your business.'

His jaw clenched. 'You little bitch,' he muttered between his teeth, his fingers biting into her flesh, 'of course it's my goddamned business! Do you think I enjoy the thought of you and my dear brother going to bed together in the afternoon?'

She saw Cara coming back across the restaurant, her step faltering as she saw the expressions on their faces, the violent tension holding Alex's lean body poised. Cara looked from one to the other of them with puzzled curiosity.

'Let go of me, Alex,' said Natasha in a low, angry voice. 'There's nothing more to say.'

Violence leapt in his eyes, and for one moment she thought he would strike her. Then he tensed, his mouth hardening, and dropped her hand angrily. He got up and left the table, walking back to his own place without looking back at her.

Natasha's body sagged with the release of tension. After that argument, she knew that everything was over between herself and Alex. We're all washed up, she thought morosely, feeling bitter tears sting the backs of her eyes.

The first day of filming dawned, and Natasha was gripped with unaccountable nerves as she dressed in her hotel room. The telephone had woken her at the crack of dawn—they were shooting on location and needed every scrap of light they could get.

She had neither seen nor heard from Alex for the past few weeks. A heavy silence had fallen over them, and she had spent many hours brooding over their last bitter argument.

At six o'clock she went down to the foyer to wait for her car. The director had laid on a car to drive her to and from the location, and she was glad because the shooting point was so far away.

She nodded with a smile to the chauffeur and slipped into the back of the car. 'Alex!' She was so surprised, it was all she could do to stop herself jumping out of the car again.

'Good morning, my dear,' he drawled in an icy voice as the car pulled away from the hotel. 'I trust you're looking forward to filming the first of our love scenes today.'

Natasha gave him a cool stare, belying the tremors running through her. 'I spoke to Marney about the sex scenes,' she told him calmly, 'and he told me you were lying.' Although they were filming a love scene, she knew it would only be a kiss, although even that sounded ominous all on its own.

Alex laughed, his voice chilling. 'You believed me?' he queried, his eyes flicking over her. 'I didn't realise you were so gullible.' He watched her with cold amusement, and she shuddered, a frisson of alarm running through her.

They rode the rest of the way in silence, and her nerves began to jangle. At last they reached the location spot, and the car pulled to a halt, surrounded by a jumble of technicians, electric cables, cameras and long trailers.

Natasha jumped quickly out of the car, breathing hard with relief while Alex walked lazily round to where she stood. 'Why don't we rehearse our love scene?' he murmured unpleasantly, trying to catch her chin, but she pulled away, glaring at him, and he laughed icily. 'It's a pity we're not sharing a trailer,' he told her. 'We could finish our rehearsal in there. But we have weeks ahead of us.' He gave her a smile. 'I'm sure we can find a way.'

She looked at him with angry eyes. 'Go away, Alex!'

He turned and walked away, leaving her to watch him with irritation. She didn't know if she could stand this day after day, it was beginning to tell on her nerves already. Her whole body was tense after their conversation in the car. What would it be like after weeks of working with him? Maybe I'll get used to it, she mused as she walked towards her own trailer.

Paulette, the wardrobe mistress, was fluttering about agitatedly. *'Non!'* she protested, her birdlike hands brushing imaginary pieces of fluff off the costume, 'I will not wait for you to finish her hair. You will wait for me, not I for you.'

Freddie, her hairdresser, was having one of his tantrums, tossing his silvery head back and rolling his eyes theatrically. 'Honestly,' he confided to Natasha, 'one does one's best, but this is the absolute end!'

Natasha smiled to herself, watching while they battled it out. Paulette and Freddie were a case of an irresistible force meeting another irresistible force! They just pushed and pushed and neither gave way. Still, they did enjoy their little arguments. Natasha had a feeling they wouldn't have it any other way.

'Arms up!' commanded Paulette briskly, yanking Natasha's dress over her head. 'Where is your head, you fool?' she asked, hunting around in the dress. 'I have lost her head! Freddie,' she turned to him with exasperation, 'can you see her head?'

'I'm in here!' said Natasha beneath masses of

folds of Paulette's magnificent silk costume. She tried to battle her way out, but it was no use.

'Don't ask me to help,' Freddie snapped, his face long-suffering and harassed. 'You've ruined her hair with your stupid costume. Find her head yourself!'

Natasha fought her way out with Paulette's help and sighed heavily as she once again saw light instead of cloth. 'It's like being eaten by a giant marshmallow,' she told Paulette, then realised what a mistake she had made.

Paulette's birdlike, unblinking eyes fastened on her. 'So!' she said with her hands on her hips, 'you call my creation a marshmallow, eh? We will see!'

Freddie went off into gales of laughter, while Natasha watched, bemused, wondering why it was her fate to be lumbered with either of them. They fought like cat and dog, and although she tried to stay out of it, she always ended up offending one of them, much to the amusement of the other.

There was a knock on the door. 'Come on, aren't you ready yet?' Marney put his head round the door. He was visiting the set for the first day of filming to make sure everything ran according to plan. 'Henry says if you're not out there in five minutes he'll slice your ears off.'

'With pleasure!' Paulette said crisply, her eyes narrowing on Freddie. 'Gladly would I give up my ears so I would not have to listen to this prattling fool any more!'

Natasha and Marney looked at each other as Freddie launched off into an attack on Paulette. Marney gave her a wink and mouthed. 'see you in five minutes' to her. Then he disappeared, closing the wooden door behind him, and left her to wait while the current argument subsided. Her make-up, luckily, was still intact, even though she had had such a struggle with her dress. At least she didn't have to call the make-up girls back in.

Freddie got back to work on her hair, pushing it this way and that, while she sat patiently in front of the mirror. When at last she was ready she sneaked out of the trailer, leaving Paulette and Freddie arguing bitterly behind her. At least they livened the place up, she decided, as she walked steadily towards the cameras. Without them, the film set would be quite dull first thing in the morning.

Alex was waiting by the director. He wore his costume, the long black leather boots making him look incredibly sexy. Black trousers were tucked into the boots, and he wore a white silk shirt un-buttoned to his waist. Natasha averted her eye from his gleaming torso.

The director, Henry Maitland, was glowering at everyone with stern bushy black eyebrows. 'You arrive at last!' he greeted her crisply. 'What kept you so long? Floods, perhaps? Doom and de-spondency raining down over your trailer?'

Natasha smiled, her cheeks dimpling. 'No, it was my hair and make-up, actually,' she said, watching the stern lordly expression become even sterner.

'So,' he said crisply, 'the unspeakable Freddie is at the bottom of it. I'll take great pleasure in slic-ing his ears off, the loathsome toad.' He cast an eagle eye over them and rested his hands on his substantial hips. 'And what are we all waiting for?'

he asked pleasantly. 'A sign from above, perhaps?'

Natasha hid a smile as she went over to her position with Alex. Henry was on form today, she noticed. He enjoyed commanding everything with a very sharp tongue, and he could slice you to ribbons within seconds if your performance wasn't up to his perfectionist standards. He seemed to think of himself as a duke, and the world of cinema was his dukedom. He saw himself as reigning nobleman. Natasha had to concede that he played his part to the hilt, and with consummate skill.

Alex and Natasha acted the scene out many times. Each time, however, something went wrong, some hitch unforeseen, and after two hours they were both getting rather irritable. They didn't seem to have quite the right feel for the scene, and it was taking a lot of time.

'That was odious!' Henry announced after the fourteenth take, his black brows wriggling about with anger. 'Can't you see your way clear, Natasha, to looking a little enthusiastic? You have all the life of a can of beans!'

Natasha wanted to crawl under a rock and die. Alex was listening to this with great amusement. It was only fair, though, she realised. Alex was playing his part superbly—it was she who was at fault. She just didn't seem able to let herself go completely with him, something kept holding her back.

They played the scene again, and Natasha found herself acting beautifully under Alex's eagle eye. He watched her all the time, his face and voice making her respond to him with fervour.

The scene neared its climax, and Natasha felt

herself become Sabrina, her whole being directed towards Lynx, and what he was saying to her. Her heart began beating faster as Alex came towards her angrily.

'I'll never love you, Lynx,' she said, her voice strained as she backed away from him, her eyes wide. Her breathless voice was real, her fear real, because she knew and understood the look in Alex's eyes.

Alex moved towards her, his black eyes malevolent. 'Maybe not,' he said, 'but your body will be mine,' and his hands reached out to drag her towards him on the cliff top, his eyes burning into hers. Her stuggles were real, her eyes wild.

'I belong to someone else,' she said in a low, breathless voice, struggling against his strong arms. 'I hate you, Lynx! I've always hated you!' She could see what he was intending to do. Theirs would not be just a screen kiss, it would be a real kiss, and she would have done anything at that moment to get away from him.

'Then hatred,' Alex said bitingly, his sharp white teeth showing through, 'is what you'll bring to my bed.'

His mouth swooped down to claim hers, and Natasha struggled desperately, feeling the bruising, punishing kiss hurt her. She pushed at his shoulders, trying to pull her head away, hitting him furiously. Alex's strong fingers bit into her neck, clamping her face in position.

'Excellent,' Alex muttered so no one else could hear. 'Keep it up and I'll always use this technique!'

Her temper flared, her eyes blazing angrily as she glared at him, hating him. She redoubled her efforts, fighting him hard as he kissed her within an inch of her life. She wouldn't be able to stand working with him like this, day after day, week after week. It would break her in the end.

'Cut! Print it!' Henry was most pleased, his eyes darting around with a superior smile in them. Natasha eyed him, wishing he had stopped the scene sooner.

Alex released her slowly, but his arms still held her in their circle. 'You'll make an actress yet, Natasha,' he drawled, his eyes laughing at her, noting the angry look on her face. He watched her in silence, his mouth curling with amusement.

Natasha controlled her temper, trying to keep her expression calm, but it didn't do much good. Inside she was furious with him for kissing her like that in front of the crew. Everyone knew they were married, of course, which was why they expected them to act even better with each other. But they didn't know all the details of their marriage, they didn't know all the bitterness that was in their past. Natasha hoped they would never find out.

She pushed away from Alex, giving him an angry look and walking away from him, her head held high. As she went she heard his mocking laughter as he laughed under his breath, but she tightened her lips and kept on walking. She refused to allow him to provoke her any further than he already had done. It would only make her look silly.

That afternoon, filming went smoothly. The first love scene completed, they moved on to a sequence where she and Alex merely talked together, without kissing each other. Natasha felt grateful for this respite. The filming was running very well, which was amazing for a first day. Usually everything that could go wrong went wrong on the first day. But things were running to schedule. Natasha had a feeling everything would go haywire tomorrow, but she didn't say anything.

'Coffee time, everyone,' said Henry at four o'clock, and waved his hand in airy dismissal. People chattered and moaned as they walked away from the cameras to sit under trees, go to trailers and drink the coffee or soft drink provided.

'Do not get that muddy!' Paulette popped up out of nowhere, wagging a slim, elegant finger at Natasha. 'I will not allow my creations to be ruined!' She watched Natasha smile and walk away, then huffed and went back in the opposite direction.

Natasha walked to the back of her trailer and sat on a chair alone. She felt very pleased with her work so far. It had been good, and even Henry seemed satisfied, which was no small task—he was a perfectionist.

It was peaceful on her own, sitting down quietly and thinking. The fear of bumping into Alex kept her from mingling with the rest of the film crew. She would rather be alone than risk facing him.

Suddenly a movement caught her eye, and she frowned, leaning forward. Who was that? she wondered, tilting her head to one side, her long blonde tresses falling over her shoulders in a cascading wave of sunlight.

She gasped as a face appeared from between the shelter of the trees. 'Roger!' Her hand flew to her mouth as she stared at him. How had he got through without a pass? How had he found out the location spot? More important—why was he here?

'Hello, Natasha,' said Roger, his eyes watching her with a shade of anxiety. He obviously wasn't certain of her reaction to his presence.

She tried to keep the stiffness out of her voice, but it was difficult. 'Why have you come here, Roger?' she asked, her face and voice guarded. He had ruined her marriage, and she doubted if she could ever forgive him for it. 'Do you want to cause more trouble, or are you just trying to make me angry?'

A tide of red stung his cheeks, and he looked away, shuffling his feet uncertainly. 'I deserved that,' he muttered under his breath, biting his lip. He looked up again, his eyes sincere. 'I came because I have to speak to you.'

Natasha sighed. She was beginning to feel sorry for him again—he looked so lost and mixed up standing there, just the way he always had. My problem, she told herself, is that I feel sorry for too many people—and just look where it gets me!

'I don't really think there's much to say after all this time, do you?' she said, her eyes running over his smooth features. 'You've waited just a little too long for baring your soul.'

He winced, his face sad, and Natasha turned her back on him, preparing to walk away. She couldn't see the point of their meeting like this.

Roger caught at her arm, his face worried. 'Please, Natasha, don't go,' he said, his voice urgent, and she turned to look at him with curiosity. He gave a rueful little smile, self-deprecating, as though he knew just how painful this was for her, and he could read her mind, seeing how futile she saw their meeting. 'I know it isn't easy, but I have to speak to you. Can you bring yourself to listen?'

She winced. Why did he put himself down like that? She might be angry with him for something he had done three years ago, but she certainly didn't despise and hate him. She had always felt very sorry for him, had understood his actions. She hadn't been pleased by them, but she had understood why it had happened.

She sighed, looking back at him. 'You'll have to be quick,' she said, her gaze darting restlessly in case Alex was watching them. She shuddered at the thought of his reactions if he saw her talking to his brother.

Roger hesitated, then shook his head. 'I'll need more time,' he told her, his eyes sincere as they held hers. 'Can you meet me tonight?'

'Don't be stupid!' she admonished, wondering how he could suggest such a thing. 'Don't you realise what Alex would do if he knew you'd been here—spoken to me?'

Roger ran a hand through his hair, sighing. 'Of course I do,' he told her, 'but it's just not going to work if I talk to you here. I have to have more time to explain things. Please, meet me tonight.'

Natasha frowned worriedly. Roger was obviously very anxious to speak to her about something. She didn't owe him a second of her time, she knew that. But all the same, something in the urgency of his voice made her think. Perhaps he was trying to make up for his actions. But then surely it was he who had contacted the press?

'Natasha?' Paulette's voice came to her from nearby, and she looked up sharply, her eyes narrowing. If Alex was near she would be in trouble.

'You'll have to go,' she said, turning to Roger quickly. 'Ring me at my hotel tonight. I'll get in at about nine.' She quickly looked round to check that Paulette wasn't coming any closer, but she saw the other woman's bubbly black head appear through the trees. 'I'm at the Negresco,' she said hurriedly to Roger.

He gave a sigh of relief and squeezed her hand. 'Thanks. I'll ring at nine.'

She bit her lip, as she heard Paulette approach. 'Go on,' she urged, pushing Roger away from her, 'quickly!' She watched him as he ran back towards the shelter of the trees and give one last wave before he disappeared out of sight.

They continued filming until well past eight o'clock, using the last of the light as best they could. When it was all over for the day, Natasha wearily went to her trailer and undressed, taking her make-up off with relief. She hated wearing make-up, it always made her feel sticky. Then she dressed in her own clothes and walked over to the car which waited silently by the film set.

Alex was nowhere to be seen, so she got into the car and waited in the back. Perhaps he had decided not to drive home with her that night. But although she secretly hoped that that was true, she knew Alex better than that. After a wait of ten minutes, she saw him appear from his trailer and make his way lazily to the car. His black hair blew in the breeze, his eyes glinting like coals. Natasha turned her head away, wondering why he still made her heart turn over with the impact of his looks.

He slid into the seat beside her. 'Good evening, Natasha,' he drawled, his eyes flicking over her. 'Have you enjoyed the day's filming?'

She raised one brow. 'It went well,' was all she said. She wasn't going to rise to the bait, and she wanted him to know it. He had done his best all day to make her angry, but she had deliberately ignored his mocking glances, deliberately ignored the malevolent gleam of his black eyes.

He rapped on the glass partition in front of them. 'Drive on,' he said as the chauffeur turned his head. The car started and they pulled away from the set, driving off down the cliff road towards Nice.

Alex was watching her steadily. 'Hungry?' he asked quietly, and at her nod a slow smile curved his lips. 'Why don't we have dinner together?'

Natasha looked at him sharply, her eyes narrowing. 'No,' she said, then added hastily, 'Thank you, but I feel rather tired after today. I think I'll just go to sleep as soon as I get in.'

He raised one dark brow. 'Don't be silly,' he murmured, watching her with his black head tilted to one side. 'You've hardly eaten today. You won't be able to work very well tomorrow on an empty stomach.'

She tightened her lips. He mustn't take her out to dinner, because if he did, what would happen to Roger? He might come looking for her, and if Alex was still around, she would find herself in terrible trouble.

She shook her head, her hands fiddling restlessly with the clasp of her bag. 'I'll be okay,' she told him, biting her lip, hoping he would let the subject drop. 'I've acted on an empty stomach before.' That was true, because when she was at drama school, she never had any money, and rather than miss out on more important things she would skimp meals and eat perhaps one sandwich a day.

Alex took her hand, a self-confident smile on his face. 'I insist,' he told her smoothly.

Natasha pulled her hand away, frowning. Whatever happened, he must drop her at her hotel and not come back. She couldn't risk him seeing Roger or even knowing that his brother had contacted her. That would be disastrous—Roger and Alex did not see eye to eye where she was concerned, and she could just see Alex becoming violent if Roger was there.

Alex frowned, his black eyes narrowing. 'You're very jumpy,' he observed, the shrewd mind ticking over quickly. 'What's going on? Have you already got a date for this evening?'

She seized on that excuse and gave him a quick smile. 'Yes,' she said, looking up at him through er lashes. 'Yes, I have another date. I'm sorry.'

Alex's eyes narrowed further. He was very still for a moment, then he asked, 'Who is it? Anyone I know?'

A chill ran down her spine at the thought of his reactions if he knew just who she was intending to see that night. His jealousy would be violent and unreasonable. He would probably knock his brother flat on the floor and cause a terrible scene.

'No,' she said in a calm voice, 'it's no one you know.' She searched around for something else to say, but her mind was shuttered, and besides, if she tried to elaborate, he would become more suspicious. It was best left as it was.

They rode the rest of the way in silence. Natasha felt uncomfortable and uneasy next to Alex, even though the car was wide. It was like being trapped in a cage with a hungry tiger. She was tense and on edge when the car finally pulled up outside her hotel.

'Goodnight,' she said quietly, getting out of the car and giving Alex a brief smile.

'Goodnight,' he murmured absently, his black eyes staring out of the window. She waited for a second, then closed the door and walked slowly up into the hotel foyer.

When she reached her room she took a quick shower, needing to wash away the day's work under the warm jets of water. She had been on the set for more than twelve hours, and she felt exhausted. Perhaps after she had had a glass of water and dressed she would feel better, more awake.

At exactly nine o'clock the telephone rang, and she nearly jumped out of her skin. She quickly went to answer it.

'It's me.' Roger's voice came over the line and

she sighed with relief. For one crazy moment she had thought it might be Alex.

'Where are you?' she asked, wondering if perhaps they were going to discuss things over the telephone.

'I'm in the foyer,' Roger said, and waited for a moment. Natasha closed her eyes. It was very lucky for both of them that Alex had driven away and not come into the hotel. If they had been delayed getting here he would almost certainly have seen Roger and put two and two together.

'Can I come up?' Roger asked. 'I won't stay long, but I really do need to talk to you, Natasha. There are so many things I want to clear up as soon as I can.'

She sighed. 'Okay. Come up. I'm in room 515.'

CHAPTER SEVEN

SHE waited for him in an overpowering silence. She could think of nothing he wanted to talk to her about, because there was no explanation necessary for his behaviour over her marriage. He had acted spitefully and out of jealousy. She understood why he had done what he had done, but she still couldn't forgive him. He didn't deserve to be forgiven; ruining other people's happiness was something unspeakable. He had acted stupidly, and now she and Alex were paying through the nose for it. All because of Roger.

A knock on the door brought her head up. She slowly went over and opened it, holding the door back for Roger to walk in.

'I'd prefer you to be quick,' she said, and her voice was sharp, although she didn't intend it to be so. 'I'm very tired, and I have a lot of work to do tomorrow.'

Roger nodded. 'Of course. I'll be as quick as I can.' He thrust his hands in his pockets, looking down at the polished toe of his shoe. He obviously found this a lot more difficult than she did. Stop feeling sorry for him! Natasha chided herself irritably.

She sighed. 'Sit down.' She gestured towards a chair nearby, and he gave her a quick relieved smile.

'Thanks,' he said, quickly sitting down. He pushed his hair back with one hand and took a deep breath. 'Well, I'll get on with it, I suppose,' he said nervously and Natasha closed her eyes with sympathy.

'You'd better have a drink first,' she said, going to the fridge and pouring him a glass of brandy. He drank it in one gulp and handed her the glass back with a smile.

He took another deep breath, then plunged in. 'It was me who rang the press,' he blurted. 'I rang them up to tell them you were married because I thought it might help. I didn't want to cause any trouble for you, I just wanted to try and help.' He looked up at her.

She frowned, wondering what on earth he was talking about. 'I knew it was you,' she told him honestly, 'I'd already worked that out.' It had been obvious the moment she heard that the press knew—she had immediately known who was behind it. Although why they had told Alex that she had phoned them, she couldn't imagine.

He gave her a troubled smile. 'I thought if I rang them and told them you were married it might bring you back together again.' He shrugged, looking down at the nails of one hand. 'I guess I thought wrong.'

You did, thought Natasha with a frown. Far from bringing them back together, it had driven them farther apart than ever.

Roger frowned too, studying her. 'You see, I realised a long time ago just how wrong I had been in separating you.' He shrugged. 'At first I thought

I was very clever because . . . well, I hated both of you, and I wanted to really get back at you.'

She gave him a wry smile. 'I know,' she said slowly. 'You were riddled with jealousy.'

Roger flushed, his face running with hot colour. He bent his head, avoiding her gaze, and linked his hands over his knees in a protective gesture. Roger was really very insecure. He lacked the confidence his brother had because he had always lived in his brother's shadow. A very threatening shadow to live in, thought Natasha grimly, when you consider Alex.

'Anyway,' he continued roughly, 'I wanted to hurt you both. So I did . . .' his voice trailed off, and he looked up at Natasha urgently. 'But I'm really sorry now, I wish to God I'd never done it.'

She believed him. The sincerity of his voice matched the urgency in his eyes, and she again felt a wave of sympathy flood out for him. He was just a lonely, mixed-up boy who didn't know how to handle other people's success.

She nodded. 'It's okay, Roger,' she said quietly, 'I do understand why it happened. Believe me, if I could change it, I would.' She spread her hands in front of her. 'But it happened, and there's nothing you or I can do to change it.'

He sighed, ruffling his hair irritably with one hand. 'But now that my plan about the press has failed——' he gestured frustratedly with his hands, 'I just don't know what to do.' He looked at her for guidance.

Natasha looked at him slowly, her face totally serious. 'You'll have to tell him, Roger,' she said softly, ignoring the look of horror that spread over his features. 'You'll have to tell Alex the truth.'

Roger looked even more horrified. His face widened along with his eyes and he stared at her open-mouthed for a few silent moments. Then he suddenly found his tongue again, and burst into a long string of sentences which left her reeling.

'I couldn't!' he spluttered. 'If I told him, he'd kill me! He's never been the same since you split up. He's permanently in a bad temper. Every time he sees me he picks on me. I always think he's going to knock me out rather than speak to me.' He shook his head violently. 'I couldn't tell him, Natasha, I just couldn't!'

She watched him with a growing irritation as he spoke to her. 'So you're just going to run away and leave us in the mess you've put us in, are you?' she said angrily, staring at him. He had created a terrible mess with his lies and his jealousy. He had tried to make up for it, but that wasn't working, and as far as she was concerned, he had better try harder.

He shook his head. 'Natasha, you don't realise what he'd do to me!' His voice was strained, frightened, and her lips tightened with anger.

'Oh yes, I do,' she told him coldly. 'He'd kill you.'

He would. Alex was quite capable of murder. Sometimes when she saw him in one of his rages, she thought he would put his hands round her throat and throttle her. He was a violent man, and he would be furious if he found out what Roger had done. But then Roger owed them at least his honesty. Even if they didn't get back together again, after all the trouble he had caused, he owed them at least that.

Roger was shaking his head, his eyes dazed. 'I'll do anything you want if you think it'll help,' he told her, 'but not that. I won't do that.'

Natasha eyed him angrily. He was still the same selfish person he had always been. He'd never change. She turned away from him, her back stiff, her head held high as she looked across the room out of the window at nothing.

'Go away, Roger,' she said quietly.

He hesitated, standing up and moving restlessly behind her. 'Natasha, I do want to help, but I just can't bring myself to tell him. Can't you understand that?'

She did understand it, but that didn't help. 'I'm sick of understanding other people when they do nothing to understand me,' she told him, her hands gripping the back of the chair in front of her. 'Go away. I'm very tired, and I don't want to listen any more.'

He made a helpless sound of frustration, which only irritated her further. 'Roger . . .' she said angrily, turning to look at him with cold eyes. He bent his head and walked quietly out of the room, closing the door behind him with a little click.

Natasha sighed, sitting down on the chair and putting her head in her hands. She rubbed her eyes tiredly. It was all too much for her. Roger had no right coming here to upset her. She had had enough punishment from both him and his brother. What more did either of them expect of her?

She stood up, her face marred by a frown and a sad expression. She felt so tired of it all, so very tired. She wandered over to the window, looking down at the sea. How nice it would be, she thought absently, to just drift along in the water down there. How peaceful and remote it would seem.

Out of the corner of her eyes she caught a movement. Oh, my God, she thought in sudden panic, Alex is down there! Roger would be leaving the hotel at any moment, and Alex would see him.

She had to stop him. She ran to her door, running full pelt down the corridor and down the stairs to the foyer. Her eyes darted crazily around, searching for Roger among the crowds of people in the foyer, but he was nowhere to be seen. She quickly darted out on to the marble steps, looking around for him.

'Roger!' she called, spotting him just outside on the pavement, 'come back in—Alex is there!' Roger turned, frowning to look at her, then his eyes moved across the road to where the long black sports car was parked.

He started to move towards her, but it was too late. Alex was opening the car door and getting out, an angry expression on his face as he locked the car and came across the road.

'Hallo, Alex,' stammered Roger, shrinking away from his brother, 'I just popped in to see Natasha for a moment—wish her luck with the film, you know.' He looked up at Alex nervously.

'So this is your date,' said Alex in a curt voice, his black eyes hard and angry. 'I wondered who it was.'

Natasha tried her best to keep calm, but the anger on his face was unmistakable. 'No,' she said in a controlled voice that belied the tremors running through her, 'Roger just dropped in for a moment. We didn't have a date together.'

Alex flicked his lashes, his gaze skimming over his brother with distaste. 'Now why should he do that, I wonder?' His upper lip curled in a sneer. 'Let me guess. You were going to figure out what to do next. It wasn't enough just to tell everyone about my marriage, was it, Roger? You wanted to cause more trouble.'

Roger looked helplessly at Natasha, his eyes pleading with her to help him. But she couldn't lift a finger even if she had wanted to. Neither of them could avoid Alex's anger, unless Roger stepped forward and told him the truth about why they had split up.

But she knew he wouldn't do that. It was pointless to even consider it. Alex would be furious, and he would probably throttle Roger. But even so, she herself didn't want Alex to become violent over this.

'Please don't cause a scene, Alex,' she said, taking a deep breath and looking straight at him. 'Roger just paid me a visit because he happened to be in Nice.'

Alex raised his dark brows. 'Really?' he enquired. 'Does he do that sort of thing often? Or have you been seeing him regularly over the last three years?'

Roger took a step towards his brother, his face troubled and anxious. 'Natasha and I haven't seen each other since she left you,' he told him in a voice that surprised her. He sounded stronger than he looked.

Alex turned his cutting gaze on him. 'What did you say?' he asked between his teeth.

Roger swallowed at the look on his face. 'Well, I just said that . . .' he began, stumbling over the words.

Alex cut him off with an icy glance. 'Get out of my sight,' he said in distaste before looking away completely. Roger swallowed with a helpless look and bolted out of the hotel, running down the marble steps and on to the street, disappearing up one of the winding side roads off the Promenade.

Alex took Natasha's arm and began leading her out of the hotel. She dragged her feet, trying to pull away from him. 'Where are we going now?' she asked with an irritable sigh.

'The villa,' came the terse reply as he pushed her into the car. 'And don't speak to me in that weary tone, or I'll slap it out of you!' He strode round to his side of the car and got in beside her. The engine burst into life and they roared away from the kerb, driving along the coast quickly.

Natasha moistened her lips with her tongue, watching the palm trees and towering buildings sweep past as they drove. Alex didn't have the right to push her around like this, but what could she do? He was stronger than her and she couldn't stop him.

'How long was he there for?' Alex asked as he jerked the gear angrily, his strong brown hand closing over it. The engine roared even louder.

Natasha shrugged, trying to remember. 'Fifteen minutes—perhaps twenty,' she told him truthfully. Roger had arrived at nine, and it wasn't half past yet. He couldn't have been there for very long at all.

He threw her an icy glance. 'Liar!' he snapped with a bite, and she frowned, looking at him with her head tilted to one side. How would he know when he arrived? Apart from that, Roger had only arrived at nine, and that meant he couldn't possibly have been there long.

'Alex, he didn't arrive until nine,' she pointed out, frowning as she watched him.

Alex gave a harsh crack of laughter. 'I saw him go into the hotel at just gone eight-thirty,' he said, and Natasha sank back into her seat, unable to believe her ears.

Alex had left her at the hotel at just after eight, and as far as she had known, he had driven back to his villa. Why on earth should he sit outside her hotel watching, waiting to see who arrived? She had told him she had a date, but surely he wouldn't go to those lengths just to see who she went out with.

'What were you doing up there for forty-five minutes?' he asked unpleasantly. 'Talking?' His voice held a sneer that made her teeth stand on edge. She tightened her lips, refusing to reply. The car jerked and swerved as they drove full pelt through the narrow, winding mountain roads.

She clung on to the edge of her seat, worried in case they jerked to a halt and she was thrown helplessly forward. Alex's driving was the result of his anger, as though he was taking it out on the car by pushing it further and further.

'I suppose you're going to tell me you're just good friends now, is that it?' he asked, swinging the wheel round as they sped round a hairpin bend.

Natasha shook her head. 'I'm not going to tell you anything.'

He threw her an angry glance, his mouth twisting bitterly. 'No, I thought as much. You're irritated when you're caught, aren't you, Natasha? You think so long as you can go to bed with men and keep your innocent image intact it'll be all right.' He turned away from her. 'Well, you're wrong. You fooled me once before, but you don't fool me now. I see you for what you are.'

She felt her lips compress angrily. How dared he speak to her like this? He had absolutely no right! The only man she had ever given herself to was him, he was the only man she had ever loved. Look where it got me, she thought with a bitterness that surprised her.

The car jerked to a stop as they arrived at the villa, and Alex turned to look at her, the black eyes burning on her. 'This is pay-up time, Natasha,' he said harshly. 'If you're giving it to every man around you I might as well take some for myself.'

She sucked her breath in at the insult, leaving her speechless for a second. 'I'll give you nothing,' she whispered shakily, her eyes wide with anger as she stared across at him. 'You don't even deserve the time of day!'

His mouth tightened into a grim line. 'Don't I?' he

asked bitingly, his hands reaching over to catch her shoulders and drag her towards him, her neck pulling back as she tried to evade him. 'In that case, if you won't give, I'll have to take!'

She fought him, struggling uselessly as he tried to hold her still, muttering under his breath at her blows as she aimed them at him.

'Stay still,' he muttered, trapping her arms against her body as he twisted her round in her seat. She aimed a blow at his head, catching him off balance, and took her chance while it was there.

Her hand fumbled with the door handle and she jumped out of the car, running along in the darkness, almost tripping over as the flat ground sloped away into a hill, filled with unseen dangers such as bushes, trees, clumps of grass that leered at her, trying to trip her up.

She heard Alex behind her, his footsteps quick as he followed her, and she quickened her pace, her heart beating loudly in her ears. If he caught up with her she would be finished; he would drag her into the villa and make love to her.

A treetrunk loomed and her foot caught on it, sending her flying forward to land with a thud on the ground, her breath pushed out of her. She stumbled up, trying to stand and run, but Alex caught up with her before she was on her feet.

'Get up,' ordered Alex, pulling her to her feet and holding on to her. His eyes travelled over her face, seeing the grass stains on the collar of her dress. 'Did you hurt yourself?' he asked flatly. 'Are you all right?'

She nodded, looking away from him, her legs shaking. 'I'm fine. I didn't see it until I fell over it.' She looked down at the offending tree trunk, cursing it and wishing there was some other way of getting out of here.

'Where did you think you were running to this time?' he demanded, his eyes burning into hers. 'There's nothing around for miles, except the sea.'

Natasha looked at him bitterly. 'I would have preferred to end up in the sea,' she said, and it was true. The thought of the calm serenity of that cool blue water made her try to struggle out of the tension she was held in by his anger.

His mouth hardened. 'Don't threaten me, Natasha. I know damned well you wouldn't take your own life. It means too much to you. All you ever think of is yourself, you don't stop to worry about other people, you just go ahead and do whatever you want to do.'

She felt her lips compress with anger. 'I wasn't threatening you,' she muttered angrily, looking away from him. 'I would prefer to be anywhere than here with you!'

His eyes flashed with temper and his fingers tightened on her. 'You don't mean that,' he said between his teeth. 'You may not love me, but at least you feel something for me. If you didn't, you wouldn't react the way you do.'

She looked up slowly, her heart beginning to thud. 'Do you care?' she asked shakily, her eyes staring up into the black depths of his.

There was a short, tense silence. The darkness seemed to make Alex look even more dark and disturbing, the silence pressing in on her as she waited for his answer.

His fingers bit into her. 'Yes,' he said, his voice thickening, 'you know damned well I do.'

His black head swooped down, his mouth taking hers in a coaxing, sensual kiss. Her hands slid to the back of his head, tangling in his hair as he kissed her. The kiss deepened, and he pressed her against him, his hands pushing into the small of her back.

'Natasha . . .' he muttered against her mouth, his lips moving hungrily over hers, his hands sliding up and down her back while she clung to him, her heart thudding violently, her pulses skipping in her ears.

His fingers tangled in her hair, brushing against the nape of her neck, and she shivered, clinging to him, her hands gripping his shoulders. His kiss deepened with a heated excitement and everything took fire, Natasha's heart racing at his touch.

Suddenly he broke away, staring at her, his face flushed, his eyes glittering. 'Why did you do it, Natasha?' he asked roughly, watching her, his hands tightening on her back.

She frowned, dazed from his kiss. 'Why did I do what?'

He raked a hand through his hair, taking a deep breath. 'Roger. Tonight at your hotel.' He swore under his breath. 'I know he was in there for forty-five minutes. What the hell were you doing? Don't expect me to believe you were just talking!'

She slowly came back to her senses, realising that he was still angry with her. Would it never end, this insane jealousy over something that didn't exist?

She frowned, looking at him curiously. 'Why were you waiting outside?' she asked, knowing what his answer would be. He wouldn't admit to his jealousy. He couldn't admit to it, because he had far too much pride to do that.

A tide of deep red ran up his neck, staining beneath his tan. 'I was curious,' he said in a low voice. 'I wanted to see who was taking you out.'

Natasha watched his face with widening eyes. 'You were jealous,' she whispered before she could stop herself.

Alex turned away, thrusting his hands into his pockets, his back to her. He looked out across the darkness in silence for a moment and Natasha watched him, her head tilted to one side.

'All right,' he said roughly, 'I was jealous. Do you blame me?' He kicked the ground beneath his feet absently, and swore under his breath. 'You preferred my own brother to me years ago, and I accepted it. I tried to turn my back on it. But now, after so long, you're still having an affair with him—and yet you never married him.' He turned to look at her. 'Why?'

She let her gaze drop away from his, her lashes sweeping her cheeks. She knew how pointless it was to try and explain from experience. Alex never took any notice of her words, merely brushed them aside with angry words of his own. She was better off not replying, at least then she would not start an arguement.

'Is it because you're still married to me?' Alex

asked roughly. 'Is that why you've never married him? If it is, tell me.' He closed his eyes briefly, as though on a spasm of pain. 'I'll give you a divorce, if that's what you want . . .' he stopped, his voice thickening. 'I won't stand in your way any more than I have already.'

Natasha felt her heart reach out to him. If only there was a way of making him listen! She wanted to take him in her arms and tell him she loved him, that she had never loved anyone else. But she knew there was no point.

'I've never wanted to divorce you, Alex,' she said at last, her eyes pained with the futility of it all. 'I didn't want to leave you in the first place.'

He stared at her in the tense silence that followed. Then he slammed his fist against a tree, resting his hand on his chin as he leaned against the tree. She watched as he bit the knuckle of his hand, and stared moodily into the darkness.

'Damn you!' he muttered angrily. 'Why can't you be honest with me? Don't you think you owe me that much?' He turned to look at her, his black eyes burning with despair. 'I gave you everything . . . everything I had, and you repaid me with a kick in the teeth. Why, Natasha? Why did you do it?'

She shook her head, unable to speak. There was so much she wanted to say, but she knew he wouldn't listen. Too much had happened between them, and they were caught in a tangled web of lies and mistrust that would eventually suffocate them.

The silence grew and eventually she spoke. 'I

can't make you believe me,' she said softly, her gaze switching back to him, studying his dark silhouette. 'All I can do is keep trying to get through to you.'

The black brows drew together in a heavy frown and he continued to stare out across the wild landscape, his sharp white teeth biting into his knuckle as he rested his hand against his mouth.

'Did he give you something I couldn't,' he asked in a low, rough voice, 'or did you just want to be free?'

She sighed painfully, running her hand through her long silken hair, pushing strands back over her shoulders. The villa was in total darkness, the grounds unlit. She stared at it, wondering how on earth things had ever got this bad between them. She would have preferred it if she had never seen Alex again. This conversation was torturing her beyond belief.

'God, Natasha,' Alex muttered in a voice raw with emotion, 'if you were in love with him I could bear it. But this . . .' he raked a hand through his hair, drawing a harsh breath. 'You don't even want him. You couldn't have wanted him three years ago or you would have gone to him. But you didn't even bother to live with him, let alone marry. You just disappeared.'

She bit deep into her lip, closing her eyes briefly. 'I never wanted him. It was only ever you.' She looked down at her hands, turning them over and twisting them absently, hardly even aware that she was doing it.

Alex clenched his fists, his mouth tightening into

an angry line. 'You just don't stop, do you?' he said bitingly. 'Everything points to it being the truth, but you don't give up. You carry on blithely protesting your innocence.'

Natasha flushed, looking away. She had known how pointless it was to try to convince him. There had been so many scenes similar to this between them, and they always ended up the same. Yet if only Roger had the guts to admit to his brother what he had done, it would all be solved within days, minutes.

'I'm sick of your innocence,' Alex told her harshly, coming towards her with anger stamped on his features, 'because I know it doesn't exist.' His eyes ran over her like searing brands. 'Beneath your white lace and big blue eyes there's a woman of fire, and I'd rather see her than the white lace.'

Natasha looked at him sharply, her eyes widening at the expression in his eyes. She swallowed, backing a little, wary of him as she tested the ground behind her with her feet, her face controlled with supreme will power.

'Take me home Alex,' she said in a quiet, low voice, trying to make him calm down by speaking to him reasonably. Their argument had angered him more than she had at first realised.

He shook his head slowly, his hands reaching for her. 'No,' he said his voice low and angry. 'Tonight I mean to find the woman I once took to my bed. I want to feel you melt against me again, Natasha. I want you tonight.' His eyes glittered down at her.

Her heart began to thud violently, and her hands

shook as she tried to push him away. 'You'll have to use force, Alex,' she said shakily, her face flooding with heat at the look in his eyes. 'I won't let you take me willingly.' But her pulses were skidding crazily already, and she knew she wouldn't be able to resist him.

'Then I'll use force,' he said bitingly, his hands slipping to her legs as he swept her up into his arms, his face next to hers. 'With pleasure.' His mouth took hers hungrily, his hard lips making her body shiver with heat and excitement. 'I'll drive my way through until you're part of me,' he muttered against her mouth before taking it hungrily until she clung to him.

He carried her inside quickly, putting her on the bed and moving down next to her, his mouth moving heatedly over hers until she moaned with sensual pleasure, her hands curling round his neck, her fingers tangling in his hair.

The long fingers moved to her breasts, splaying over them, his index finger brushing her nipple through the material before sliding her dress off her shoulders and discarding it on the floor. His fingers trembled as he unbuttoned his shirt, flinging it away carelessly.

'Natasha . . .' he groaned into her mouth as her fingers tangled in the wiry black hair of his chest, running her fingertips over his hot flesh until excitement made her moan against him.

They twisted together on the bed, the rough hair of his thighs against her own drove her into a frenzy. His hands moved hungrily over her naked body, moving down to her thighs, and she arched against him, her fingers caressing his hips with abandon.

Alex's head moved down, his mouth closing over her breast, his sharp white teeth nibbling her skin while she twisted beneath him, her jaw clenched tight, her eyes wild with excitement. After so long the release would be explosive, the pleasure a sweet, torturing agony.

'You're mine,' he bit out thickly as he drove into her, his hands biting into her as she moved against him, his eyes glittering down at her black and malevolent.

Her nails dug into his smooth back, raking down to his waist. Her breath was coming in short piercing gasps, her heart thudding like a steam hammer, her face flushed and hot with excruciating pleasure.

'I hate you . . .' he muttered hoarsely, his breath coming in agonising gasps, his heart hitting his chest violently as his fingers bit into her flesh, 'Oh God, I hate you!'

Natasha felt something snap inside, and she drove against him in sweet piercing movements, her head spinning, her limbs moving like liquid fire. 'Alex!' she gasped unconsciously against his black hair. 'Alex . : .'

Then he was driving into her, his face contorted with pleasure, gasping her name over and over again as he filled her, became part of her, his hands and body claiming her as his own.

Peace settled over them, beauty of fullfilment lulling them into a soft haven where only time would bring the hatred back again. For the next few minutes they were deeply contented, happier than they had been for years, each clinging to the other without thought, as though if they let go the mirage would collapse and the bitterness would rise again.

CHAPTER EIGHT

NATASHA blinked, sweat making her eyelids heavy, her lashes damp against her cheeks. She looked at Alex's black head resting on her shoulder, the damp curve of his bronzed back. How did this happen? she asked herself. They had been arguing, talking to each other. Natasha had known all along how it would end up, but she had felt powerless.

They had both wanted each other with equal intensity. Now it was over, she felt the warmth and contentment leave her, replaced by a feeling of sadness, a sense of loss. Her hands rested on his shoulders, smoothing his damp flesh beneath her fingertips. She had always known how much Alex wanted her, had always known that the powerful physical attraction between them was too strong to be killed by arguments, too strong to be killed by lack of trust. She had thought perhaps the knowledge of what had gone between them would serve to make one or the other of them turn away, unable to go through with it. But she had been wrong.

The intense desire between them was still as explosive as ever, if not more so. Their bitter quarrel had only served to fire that desire, making it burn more intensely, making them reach new heights, smashing down all the barriers Natasha had tried to put in his way.

Alex had not been lying when he had said he

would drive his way through until he was a part of her. He had driven deep into her soul, making her ache with the need to have him back again. Now she felt only pain, because she knew that in a few moments he would turn on her again. His own lack of trust in her was hurting him far more badly than it was her. At least she had the comforting knowledge that she was being wrongly accused. Alex was going through hell picturing his wife with another man—which must hurt him more than she could imagine.

She frowned, trying to put herself in his place. How would she feel imagining him in another woman's arms? Who do I know, she thought, who's like a sister to me? Her mind instantly flashed a picture of her friend Ruth to her, and she winced, her eyes closing briefly. She wouldn't be able to forgive him, she knew, if he slept with Ruth. It was too horrible even to imagine.

Alex stirred beside her, raising his black head slowly and looking down at her with a straight face.

They looked at each other in total silence for a few long seconds, then Alex said, 'How do you feel?' abruptly, his eyes hooded by heavy lids.

Natasha looked away for a second, unable to meet his gaze any longer. 'I'm fine,' she said softly, watching her hands as they rested still against his shoulders.

His gaze flicked over her, his face expressionless. 'Did I hurt you?' he asked in a curiously flat voice, and she looked up at him slowly, moistening her lips with her tongue.

'A little,' she admitted huskily, remembering the way his hands had ripped her clothes away, 'at first.' But after that first violent assault on her body, pleasure had followed swiftly until they had been carried to soaring heights, and he had hurt her no more. Their lovemaking had been a shattering experience; each taking what the other gave, pushing each other to the brink of ecstasy.

'I'm sorry,' he said deeply, studying her with those black eyes. Then he gave her a rueful smile. 'I was a little out of control.' He shrugged, raising his brows.

Natasha returned his smile, unable to help herself. 'I noticed,' she teased, her voice becoming softer as she remembered the almost crazed expression on his face as he took her, the raw emotion in his voice as he called her name over and over again.

There was a little silence, then Alex slowly rolled away to lie next to her, his arms sliding around her, making her feel warm, secure. Perhaps he would forgive her, perhaps he would take her back. But even as she thought it, she knew it wouldn't happen. He was too proud. He would never consider taking her back unless he knew that she had never been unfaithful to him. And if Roger didn't confess, there was no chance of that happening.

Natasha rested her hands on his arms, her head on his chest. 'So what happens now?' she asked huskily.

She felt him shrug, then he gave a heavy sigh. 'I don't know, Natasha. It's too soon to even think about.' He stroked her hair with one long hand, holding her softly against him. 'Let's sleep on it. In the morning we won't feel biased by what's happened tonight.'

She raised her eyes, looking up at him. 'I want to talk about it now, Alex,' she said quietly.

His hand stopped stroking her hair for a second. 'What good would it do?' he asked deeply. 'Everything has been said before. We both know that what happened three years ago can never be resolved.'

Her eyes were pained as she studied him. 'It could be if you would only listen,' she said, a tinge of bitterness creeping into her voice, 'but instead you insist on treating me the way you do, when there's no reason for it.'

There was a little silence, then he said, 'Tonight was beautiful. Let's not spoil it by having an argument.' He looked at her in the cradle of his arms. 'There's nothing to be gained, and so much to lose.'

Natasha's mouth compressed into a tight line. 'You have nothing to lose,' she told him. 'You've already made up your mind about me. But I've lost to you all the way down the line, and now you want to make me lose again.' It was so unfair.

There was another silence, and she listened to his breathing as she lay against his chest. Then he reached out one hand and turned off the light with a click.

'Go to sleep, Natasha,' he said flatly, closing the conversation before it had begun.

She lay awake in his arms for what seemed like hours. Slowly, he fell asleep, and she lay perfectly still, listening to the sound of his breathing. The room was quiet, peaceful, but she was filled with a deep, gnawing sadness that was unbearable.

She slipped out of his arms at three o'clock in the morning. Dressing silently, she left the villa and vanished quietly into the night. She took the darkened road down into the nearest village, walking along without her shoes, her bare feet sensitive as she stepped on one or two rough stones.

Her face was stiff, expressionless as she found a taxi and got into the back seat. It was only as they drove silently into Nice that she felt a solitary tear slip over her lashes to run into her mouth.

Her lips trembled, and she fought back the urge to cry. She had expected Alex to be more responsive after love, more sensitive, but she had been wrong. The morning would have brought nothing but further arguments.

By the time she got to her hotel room she knew she would have to leave. She couldn't work with Alex. She couldn't look at his face again. He hated her, and would only continue punishing her.

I'll go back to London, she thought wearily, closing her tear-wet eyes as dawn came creeping through her window.

She awoke late; too late to go to the film set. Her telephone had been left off the hook because she hadn't wanted to be disturbed, and the film crew hadn't been able to wake her. People came and banged on the door, but she had locked it from inside, and refused to answer. Eventually they gave up.

She got up at eleven and dressed quickly. She would have to go to see Marney, and explain why she was leaving *The Devil's Mistress*. He deserved a better explanation than she was going to give him, but she couldn't face talking about Alex.

Marney was gibbering with rage. 'Are you crazy?' he demanded, pacing up and down the borrowed office, chain-smoking like mad and waving his hands about. 'You can't just up and leave like you're on holiday! This is work, Natasha, not Fairyland!'

Natasha bent her head and shrugged. She felt numb inside. 'Sorry, Marney, but I've told you—I can't work with him.' She looked up with troubled eyes. 'I want you to get me out of the contract, out of the picture,' she announced softly.

'What!' Marney nearly had a heart attack, his face incredulous and almost apoplectic. 'You can't do this to me! They'll crucify me, they'll string me out for the vultures to peck at!' He looked at her accusingly. 'Is that what you want?'

She raised pain-filled blue eyes to his. 'I've already been crucified, Marney,' she said shakily. It was true. Alex had practically put her on the rack over the last few weeks, and she couldn't face any more of it.

Marney stopped, biting his lip. He sighed, and collapsed into a chair, which nearly collapsed with him. 'Oh well,' he muttered, 'I guess you know what you're doing.' He looked across at her.

'I'm going back to London,' she told him, standing up and walking over to where he sat. 'I'll read some scripts while I'm there, see if there's anything around at the moment.'

Marney gave her a wry look. 'Are you kidding? If you walk out on this no one will touch you with a barge pole for at least the next six months.' He shook his head wearily, mopping his brow. 'Sure you won't change your mind?' he asked hopefully. 'I mean, there's still time . . . no one knows except you and me yet.'

Natasha shook her head, her mouth tightening. 'I won't change my mind,' she said, her brain flashing a picture of Alex's violent face into her mind. She looked back at Marney. 'I wish I didn't have to leave you to clear up the mess, but you're the only one who can handle it.'

He sighed, standing up and going over to light yet another cigarette with the dirty box of matches on his desk. He began pacing up and down the room again, muttering.

'You'll make yourself ill,' she told him worriedly.

He groaned. 'I am ill. I'm having multiple cardiac arrests, and what are you doing? I'll tell you— standing there bright as a button telling me you're going trooping back to London!'

She frowned anxiously. Poor Marney, it wasn't fair on him. But then it wasn't fair on her either. She wouldn't be able to work with Alex on the film, she knew that. From the moment he had been announced to play Lynx she had known it.

She slipped her jacket on and moved towards the door. 'I have to catch my plane,' she told him. 'Tell them I can't work with my ex-husband any longer. Give them the money back—give them

anything they want. I don't care about the money,
I just want to go home.'

'She doesn't care about the money!' Marney
sighed on a groan of physical pain. 'You haven't
seen the lawsuits piling up yet, that's why you don't
care about the money.' He ravaged his hair with
one hand, pacing furiously, then he stopped and
looked at her with narrowed eyes. 'Did you say *ex*-
husband?'

Natasha nodded slowly. 'I'm divorcing him as
soon as I get back to London.'

Marney whistled below his breath, his face
serious. 'He's not going to take kindly to that,' he
muttered, and came towards her, looking down at
her worriedly. 'You sure you'll be all right? Where
are you going? The flat?'

She nodded. 'If you can't reach me there, I'll be
at Ruth's.' Ruth was her closest friend, and the
only person likely to be able to handle Alex. Alex
and Ruth would be perfectly matched for a good
battle.

Marney's eyes were shrewd. 'Wise choice!' he
laughed a little. 'Boy, even I wouldn't want to meet
Ruth on a dark night. That lady packs one hell of
a verbal punch!'

Natasha smiled. Ruth could handle anyone; she
was a very capable lady. 'I'll ring you when I can,'
she told Marney, and opened the door with a
smile.

Marney patted her cheek. 'Good luck, kid,' he
said affectionately.

Natasha left his office and went straight back to
the hotel. She packed as quickly as she could, leav-

ing her shampoos and other unnecessary items behind. The desk called a taxi for her, and she waited patiently for it to arrive while the porter took her baggage downstairs.

The telephone rang while she was waiting in her room. Thinking it would be the desk with her taxi, she went quickly to answer, leaning casually over the silk-covered bed.

'Hello?'

'Where the hell did you get to?' Alex's voice cracked over the line like a whip. She jumped inside, afraid that he knew she was leaving, afraid he might try to stop her.

'I had an appointment,' she said in a quiet voice, trying desperately to keep her tone cool and well modulated.

There was a little silence, then Alex said huskily, 'Natasha, I must see you.'

She was surprised by the tone of his voice. She frowned, tempted for a split second. Then she remembered his vicious attacks on her, and her mouth tightened. She gripped the receiver with a tight fist, controlling herself.

'I'm sorry, Alex,' she said stiffly, 'I have to go.' She replaced the receiver, hearing his voice come back across the line before they were cut off. She stared at the phone in silence for several moments.

What had he meant, he had to see her? To talk again? She shook her head unconsciously. She didn't want to go over everything again; it was too painful even to consider. The porter arrived back in her doorway and rapped politely on the door. Her taxi had arrived. Slowly she went down to the front of the hotel, and drove to Nice Airport.

London welcomed her in the glittering heat of a summer afternoon. The tarmac shimmered and waved, making the buildings undulate like a mirage before her, almost as though they were waving hello to her. Natasha closed her eyes, feeling a pang of sadness. She was home, but she was alone.

She managed to find a taxi outside, which was lucky because at lunchtime the usual row of black taxis dwindled under the heavy demand of lunchtime flights.

' 'Ere, you're that film star, aren't you?' the driver asked, grinning as he recognised her, and she returned his smile.

She nodded, and got into the taxi with a smile. He stowed her cases in the front and they sped away from the airport, driving along the motorway with green fields on either side of them.

The driver slid the glass partition back. 'Saw you on the telly the other day,' he told her cheerfully as they drove past the Three Feathers. 'Didn't think much of the film—some daft story about a murderer.' Natasha smiled as she listened to him continue. 'Downright silly if you ask me, but you weren't bad in it.' He grinned at her in the rearview mirror.

Natasha turned her head and looked out of the window. It was good to be home, but there was an emptiness inside her that made her feel hollow and very sad.

Everything was so pointless all of a sudden. All she had ever wanted was a man who loved her, whom she loved too. But although she had found him for a brief, idyllic period of time, he had been snatched away from her in a whirlpool of bitterness and deceit.

I'm a one-man woman, she thought morosely, looking for the man who got away. She felt a tear trickle down her cheek and brushed it away angrily. Her heart ached with emptiness, her jaw hurting from the tight rein of control she was exercising over herself.

'He's not worth it, love,' the driver's voice came to her as they drove over the Hammersmith flyover, 'You take my advice—forget him.' He gave her a smile in the mirror.

She hadn't realised she had been crying so much. Her face was wet with tears, she found, as she brushed a hand over her cheeks. She licked her fingers absently, tasting the salt water on her tongue.

They reached Knightsbridge, and she leaned forward to give her address. Her flat loomed up ahead, the white and black façade of the pillared house seeming somehow both familiar and distant at the same time. She had been away too long, gone through too much since she last came home.

She set up divorce proceedings the next day. Her lawyer asked her the minimum of personal questions, telling her that it would be easy to get the divorce through given the circumstances and time of separation.

She spent the following two weeks shopping quietly in London, visiting one or two old friends and reading scripts at home in her flat. It was peaceful there, and she was not bothered by hungry reporters with painful questions.

One day the doorbell rang when she was expecting a friend. She went to the door, unprepared for the shock that was in store for her.

Alex pushed the door back with the flat of his hand, striding into the flat with an angry expression. Natasha backed in surprised disbelief, her eyes startled.

'Is this some sort of joke?' Alex demanded, flinging a thick envelope down on the telephone table with a thud.

She looked at it, realising it contained the divorce papers. 'How did you find out where I lived?' she asked, trying to keep as calm as possible.

'I've got a tongue in my head,' he said curtly. He took a step towards her, his face brooding. 'Well? What the hell gives you the idea that you have grounds for divorcing me?'

She forced herself to remain calm and clearheaded. 'We've been separated for long enough, Alex,' she told him. 'There's nothing you can do about it.'

'Oh no?' he came back angrily, his mouth tightening as though she had blatantly challenged him with her words. 'What makes you so sure about that?'

She met his stare, her blue eyes expressionless. 'My lawyer told me the case would go through without a hitch. The separation is grounds enough on its own.'

His eyes flashed. 'Really?' he said bitingly. 'I suppose you forgot to mention the fact that you're an adulterous bitch. No doubt you didn't want to muddy your good name.'

Natasha flushed hotly, the colour stinging her cheeks. 'It wouldn't have made any difference what had happened. A separation of over two years is quite adequate.' Her mouth compressed with anger. 'And I wasn't unfaithful,' she reminded him.

He gave a harsh crack of laughter, his skin taut across his hard bones. 'Of course, you're too bloody innocent for that,' he said sarcastically, and came towards her with fury in his eyes. 'But you don't like to hear the truth, do you? You prefer to hide behind your public image, pretending to be sugar and spice and all things nice.'

Her lips trembled, her hands clenching into fists. 'Get out!' she said angrily. 'Get out and don't come back. I never want to set eyes on you again!'

'Too bad,' he bit out between his teeth, 'because I'm not going to let you get away with this. You're not getting your divorce without a fight from me.'

She was breathing unsteadily, her eyes hating him as she stared at him. 'And how do you propose to stop me?'

A malevolent smile curled his lips. 'I'll go into court and tell them just what a promiscuous little whore you are.'

Her hand shot out, a resounding slap ringing through the air as her hand connected with his cheek. Alex was stunned for a moment, shocked by the force of that slap. His head jerked back, and he stared at her for a moment.

He raised his hand, violence leaping in his eyes, and she thought he was going to slap her back. She shrank away from him, her face whitening with fear.

'Hell!' he muttered thickly, and his hand dropped to his side. He turned, picking up the envelope from the table and slammed out of the door without another word.

Natasha went into the living room with tears running down her face. She mustn't allow herself to get upset about it. She had known what Alex's reaction would be when he saw she was divorcing him. She ought to have expected it. But she hadn't realised he would find out where she lived.

Now he knew, of course, he would probably be back. She couldn't stay in her flat any longer. She would have to go somewhere else and hide until it had blown over.

She went over to her writing desk and began to write a letter to Marney, telling him where she was going. She would go to Ruth's, spend some time with her. She couldn't possibly go to her aunt's—it would be too unbearable to visit that house again. Too many memories were locked inside it.

The next two days were spent arranging her stay with Ruth and settling all the business she had in London. Ruth lived in a suburb on the outskirts of London. Natasha didn't want to have to come up to London again for any reason, because she might bump into Alex.

Henry Maitland, the enraged director, sent her a telegram. 'You unspeakable wretch, stop. May you rot in hell, stop. Henry.' She laughed when she read it, picturing his angry face when he found out she had left the film. But anger or no, he would appreciate why she had gone. He himself had been through a painful experience with his wife, and although he never showed his feelings on the surface, they were there, glimmering just below.

She arrived at Ruth's in the late afternoon, having got a taxi from the station. Pressing her finger on the doorbell, she was immediately aware of noises coming from the white-painted house as people ran about and a dog woofed excitedly.

The door opened and a mad jamboree of faces and eyes appeared. Ruth's black head popped round the door, clamping both hands on her two children's shoulders as they jostled.

'About time too!' said Ruth bluntly, her blue eyes boring into Natasha unwinkingly. 'I wanted to do some shopping, but I had to wait for you. Where do you think you've been?'

Natasha waved at the children, who waved merrily back. 'The train was delayed,' she explained.

The children, two grass-stained ragamuffins, jumped all over Natasha. 'Mummy says you're a pest,' the eldest, Jonathan, informed her with glee, his dark hair an unruly mop over his shiny eyes. 'She said she was going to bash you over the head with a saucepan when you got here.'

Natasha hid a smile, raising her brows at Ruth. 'Did she?' she said.

Ruth glared at the boy. 'Jonathan, how many times have I told you not to repeat what I say?' she demanded, hovering over him like a big black crow.

Jonathan giggled and tugged on Natasha's sleeve. 'What do you call a thief who steals meat?'

Natasha grinned at him. 'I don't know. What do you call a thief who steals meat?'

'A beef-burglar!' Jonathan and his brother went off into peals of laughter, jumping about all over the hall and bringing out their book of jokes, which Ruth snatched away irritably.

'Outside!' she commanded sternly, leading them by their ears to the back door and closing the door behind them. Natasha brought her case in and went into the kitchen close on her heels.

Ruth's kitchen was immaculate. A place for everything and everything in its place, was her motto when doing the housework. Not a dish was out of place, not a crevice left unswept. The floor was clean enough to eat off, and the whole place smelt deliciously of pine.

'So,' Ruth handed Natasha a steaming cup of tea, 'what exactly happened between you and Alex? You seemed happy enough to leave everything as it was, but now you've suddenly decided to divorce him.'

Natasha didn't want to talk about it. She tried to avoid Ruth's questioning, but her friend was like a ferret, and burrowed around digging things up and trying to make Natasha answer them.

She spent the next two hours trying to convince Ruth that she really wasn't going to tell her anything about her marriage. It was over, and that was all she would hear. But Ruth did not give up

on something once she had her mind set on it. She
bullied and huffed, puffed and threatened, waved
her hands about in the air, but Natasha didn't
budge an inch. It hurt too much to talk about Alex.
It hurt to even think of him.

'Talk about secretive!' Ruth complained to her
husband James when he arrived home from work.
'I'd need a tin-opener to get anything out of her
mind—she's worse than a can of pilchards!'

James was amused. He listened to Ruth's com-
plaints with a bemused smile, leaning casually on
the doorjamb as she muttered indignantly all over
the kitchen.

'Well done!' James mouthed to Natasha when
Ruth wasn't looking, and Natasha giggled, her eyes
twinkling.

Ruth turned round and caught them smiling.
'Really!' she said with a sniff, her nose in the air.
'You're like children sometimes!' and she carried
on briskly peeling the potatoes.

James excused himself calmly, saying he wanted
to do some work in his shed. He gathered a few
things up and wandered down to the bottom of the
garden, avoiding the children as they nearly
knocked him over, and went into his shed.

Ruth watched out of the kitchen window. 'That
man's obsession with his shed is becoming
nothing short of disgusting,' she said sourly, and
glared at Natasha in case she dared to say anything. Ruth didn't mean it, of course, she was
just getting her own back on James. They were
perfectly matched.

Natasha finally got to bed at eleven. It was the

first time she had been alone all day, and she was grateful for the peace of her quiet bedroom.

She unpacked her clothes and slipped into bed with a tired yawn. Her mind was alive, however, and she couldn't sleep for a long time. She kept thinking of Alex, going over everything he had said. He wasn't going to give her her divorce, that had been made obvious. She didn't understand why, though. Surely, if he hated her as much as he said he did, he would be glad to be rid of her?

She frowned, her brow wrinkling with thought. It was so difficult trying to see inside his head. He had made it clear that he believed the worst of her, so why should he be angry that she was divorcing him?

His pride, perhaps? Or was it more than that? She tried to quell the feeling of hope inside her by telling herself that even if he did love her as much as that, he wouldn't take her back because he could never forgive her for what had supposedly happened.

She gave up trying to figure him out in the end, and relaxed her tired mind, falling asleep relatively easily once she had made up her mind to do so.

CHAPTER NINE

THE days slowly drifted away until Natasha realised she had been at Ruth's for a week. She spent her time playing with the children, taking them for walks in the park, pushing them on the swings and roundabout. They were lively company, and seemed to have dozens of friends in the neighbourhood, many of whom Natasha was kindly introduced to. Their grinning pixie faces popped up from behind wastepaper baskets, park benches, shop doorways; all leaping out on to Jonathan and Sebastian at the first opportunity. They reminded her of a little network of moles, spying on the adults who lived in a different world from their own.

When she wasn't with the children she sat and talked to Ruth, while Ruth worked around her busily. She refused all offers of help from Natasha, giving her frosty glares if she tried to so much as pick up a piece of fluff. Ruth's house was her castle, and she had no qualms about throwing people off the battlements if they tried to interfere in her smooth-running system.

'What are you going to do about him?' she asked one lazy afternoon while they were sitting in the kitchen drinking coffee. 'I mean, you're welcome to stay here until you start to disintegrate, but I'm sure you wouldn't want to do that. You have a career, don't forget.'

Natasha looked up, frowning. 'I hope I'm not in the way, Ruth,' she said worriedly, because that thought hadn't occurred to her until just now. She had had too many other things on her mind.

Ruth gave her a dry smile. 'Don't worry. If you were I'd shove you out into the street. You'd soon know if we were fed up with you.' She gave her a frank stare. 'Surprising, really, that we're not fed up yet. Your face is long enough to make a hyena sad!'

Natasha grimaced, feeling hot colour sweep into her cheeks. 'I didn't realise it showed quite so much,' she mumbled into her coffee cup, avoiding Ruth's eyes.

Her friend shrugged. 'It doesn't always. But you have an intriguing habit of staring into space for hours on end. I thought maybe we had a damp patch in the walls, but then I realised you were miles away, on some other planet.' She laughed. 'With Alex, no doubt!'

Natasha bit her lip. She had spent so much time thinking, wondering how Alex was, where he was and what he was doing. It hadn't occurred to her that anyone would notice.

At that moment, two things happened to make their conversation end. The telephone rang and the children came bursting into the room in a jumble of arms and legs. Ruth dashed off to answer the phone, Sebastian ran into the kitchen for crisps, and Jonathan followed hot on his heels. 'I want some!' he bellowed, grabbing a handful of crisps from Sebastian, who pinched his arm crossly.

'Hallo,' said Jonathan, waving at Natasha. 'We've got something in this kitchen that will make all your dreams and wishes come true.'

Natasha raised her brows, grinning. 'What's that?'

'An automatic wishing machine,' said Jonathan, and had hysterics all over the floor. He pinched some more of Sebastian's crisps and dodged a punch from his younger brother.

Natasha smiled at their boisterous antics. 'You look as though you've been having fun,' she observed, her gaze sweeping over their muddy clothes. 'What have you been doing?'

Jonathan grinned. 'We went to the park with Nicholas Barrett. He's got a toy machine-gun and we played shooting all the dogs.' He grinned even more at Natasha's expression of horror. 'Then he shot me and I fell off my bike like they do on T.V. and I cut my leg.' He rolled his trouser leg up quickly and brought it over for inspection. 'Look, it's all bloody.'

Natasha swallowed. 'Very nice. Take it away, you gruesome child!' she said, looking away from his leg, which wasn't cut so much as bruised all over. 'Go and wash it in the bathroom.'

Ruth came back in and shrieked when she saw his leg. 'You horrible monster!' she exclaimed, bustling him into the bathroom. 'You should have washed it at once!'

Natasha waited, bemused, for her to reappear a moment later. 'There's someone on the phone for you,' Ruth told her. 'Don't worry—it's not Alex. You can take it in there.' She waved absently with one hand before going back to scrub the now wailing Jonathan.

Natasha went into the living room, ignoring the plaintive cries for help from the bathroom. Ruth's children were very lovable, but one had to draw the line somewhere. She shuddered as she remembered Jonathan's leg.

She picked up the telephone, aware that it could only be one person. After all, only one person knew she was here, and that at least was a relief of sorts.

'Hallo, Marney,' she said, sitting down on the chair next to the telephone. She knew why he had rung her, of course—to let her know in horrible detail precisely how much International would be sueing her for. He had a grim little mind at times.

'My desk,' bellowed Marney, 'is covered from head to toe with lawsuits!' Natasha heard paper rustling about in the background and smiled to herself. It was easy to imagine his irritated face.

'But, Marney,' she reminded him calmly, 'your desk hasn't got a head,' and smiled as another outburst came from him, the line crackling angrily. She held the mouthpiece away from her ear until he had calmed down a little.

Eventually he sighed. 'Listen, Natasha, that's not the reason I called. Something else has happened.' He paused. 'I thought you should know about it.'

She frowned, her brow knitting in thought. He knew that she would hand all business matters to him or her lawyer, and leave them to sort it out. She herself didn't like handling money because it frightened her, whatever it was. She preferred other people to do it, take care of it for her. That meant his problem was personal—to do with her, and she didn't like the sound of that.

'What is it?' she asked slowly, her mind ticking over with incredible speed.

'Your ex-husband,' he said bluntly. 'He burst in here the other day, frightened my secretaries out of their wits and threatened to crack my head open like a walnut if I didn't tell him where you were.'

Natasha felt her heart stop for a second, then burst back into life. 'What did you do?' she asked, knowing the answer already, feeling her pulse throb dangerously in her temples.

'Are you kidding?' Marney was amazed at her question. 'I told him Ruth's address—I value my neck! I'm sorry, kid, but I thought you ought to know. Besides, I figured Ruth could handle him for you.'

After Marney had hung up Natasha sat in the living room for a long time, her face filled with frozen disbelief. If Alex knew her address he would be making his way towards her at this moment. She hated the idea of having to run away again, but she had very little choice.

She went back into the kitchen to tell Ruth what had happened. Ruth was scathing, her tone irritated with Natasha. She felt that it was time she faced up to her responsibilities, and one of them was letting Alex know in no uncertain terms that their marriage was over for good.

Natasha tried to argue with her, but Ruth's mind was made up. She expected Natasha to stay where she was, and that as far as she was concerned was that. But Natasha wasn't going to stay. She had already made up her mind that she was going.

But where? She went up to her room and sat down on the bed, her head resting on her hands. She had plenty of friends in London, but she didn't want to descend on them, bringing the prospect of an argument with Alex hand in hand along with her. That wasn't fair.

If she went back to her flat, she would be running the risk of him finding her there. She could always go to her aunt's but she dismissed the idea with a grimace. Much as she was grateful to her aunt for bringing her up, she knew she couldn't go back there.

Aunt Stella hadn't changed; her telephone conversation in Nice had proved that. Natasha loved her and felt deep sympathy towards her, but she couldn't bring herself to go back there. It would hold too many painful memories for her. She would prefer to face Alex.

She sighed, standing up. There was only one thing for it: she would have to book in at an hotel somewhere. Not in London, because Alex would find her there. It would have to be somewhere different. She began to pack her bags, trying to think of a place she could go to where Alex wouldn't think of looking.

It sounded absurd, but she would have to sneak out when Ruth wasn't looking. Natasha giggled to herself. It was quite an adventure really, she decided, trying to cheer herself up. But somehow her heart wasn't in it.

She went back downstairs to the kitchen, pretending to be calm and unruffled. Ruth eyed her sharply, aware that she had been upstairs for rather a long time.

'Don't think I can't see devious little plots hatching up there,' she said bluntly, pointing to her head. 'I'm not blind, you know.'

Natasha looked at her with wide eyes. 'Me?' she queried, sitting on one of the kitchen chairs. 'I've just been reading a book in my room. Anyone would think I'd been doing something illegal!'

Ruth's eyes narrowed. 'Book my foot!' she snorted, her movements brisk as she washed the pork chops and popped them in the oven. 'You've been plotting—I know that look of old. Honestly, you're worse than Jonathan sometimes!'

The doorbell rang and they both froze, then Natasha looked at Ruth with pleading eyes.

'If it's him,' she said shakily, 'don't let him in.' She caught Ruth's arm. 'Please!'

Ruth looked down at her for a moment, then nodded briskly. She went out of the kitchen leaving Natasha alone, her back stiff, her face tightly controlled. Natasha heard the door open, and Ruth's bossiest voice ring out from the hall.

Her heart punched at her chest as she heard Alex answer in a dark voice. Her hands twisted together and she swallowed, trying to hear the words. He wouldn't force his way in, surely?

'If I were a man,' Ruth promised angrily as footsteps rang out down the hall, 'I'd knock you into the middle of next week!' Alex was heard to mutter something in reply as he came nearer to the kitchen.

Natasha sprang to her feet, her eyes darting around in confusion. She tried to open the back door and run out, but as she reached for the handle, Alex loomed in the doorway. He looked dark and brooding in a well cut black suit, his face grim.

'I have to talk to you,' he said deeply, and his eyes were hooded, masking his thoughts and feelings.

Natasha flushed in confusion, her eyes darting to Ruth's, pleading for her help.

'She doesn't want to talk to you,' Ruth informed him angrily, her face getting sharper the more she got irritated. 'She just wants you to go away.' Her nose pointed at him threateningly, her pinched white face showing her unwinking blue eyes vividly.

Alex slid his hands in his pockets, his eyes not moving from Natasha's face. 'I haven't come to fight with you, Natasha,' he said, 'I've come to talk to you.'

She looked away, her mind darting around helplessly. How was she supposed to believe him, after all this time? He had hurt her so much already, she didn't think she was prepared for more.

A stain of red ran along his hard cheekbones. 'Please,' he said, his black eyes holding hers.

Natasha looked helplessly at Ruth, who shrugged and said, 'On your own head be it,' and went out of the kitchen, leaving them alone together.

Natasha bent her head, her lashes sweeping her cheeks. 'I'm not going to change my mind about the divorce,' she said huskily. 'It's still going through.'

Alex drew a deep breath. 'I just want you to hear me out,' he told her, 'then you can decide whether or not to carry on with it.'

She nodded, lacing her hands together. She knew he could have nothing to say that would change her mind. If he still believed she had been unfaithful to him there was no chance of their ever living together.

Alex ran a hand through his hair, watching her steadily across the room. 'Natasha,' he said slowly, 'I spoke to Roger a few days ago.' He raised his head, looking at her openly. 'I know now that he was lying about the two of you. I know you didn't sleep with him.'

Her eyes widened, her heart starting to beat faster. She stared at him in shocked amazement for a few silent moments. Then she recovered her tongue.

'How did you find out?' she stammered, her hands spreading as she frowned. 'Did he tell you? Did he come to you with the truth?' She could hardly believe it of Roger. He had finally owned up to his responsibilities.

Alex grimaced. 'Unfortunately, no.' He gave her a rueful half smile. 'I had to beat it out of him.'

Her eyes widened further. Poor Roger! But then he had been given his choice a long time ago, and he had taken the wrong road. 'You didn't hurt him?' she asked anxiously, sympathy coming through yet again.

Alex shook his head. 'No more than he deserved.' He drew a shaky breath, his mouth hardening. 'When I think of the anguish he's caused, I could quite cheerfully knock his face through the back of his head!'

Natasha looked down at her hands, her mind confused. Even though he now knew the truth, she still felt frightened of him. The violence was still there, in every line of his body.

Alex continued, 'After the last time I saw you in Nice,' his voice became husky, 'when I made love to you at the villa,' he watched the hot colour seep into her cheeks and carried on quickly, 'I knew I couldn't go on the way we were.'

She raised her eyes to meet his. 'So did I,' she said quietly, because that was why she had left the film.

'I was going to speak to you about it the following morning, but,' he watched her steadily, 'when I woke up you'd gone. I went through hell, wondering why you'd left in the night. I couldn't reach you at your hotel, you weren't on the set, and no one knew where you were.'

Natasha sighed. 'I went to see Marney,' she told him. 'I'd already decided to leave the film.'

Alex nodded. 'I was going to ask you to come back to me,' he said deeply. 'I knew I'd had enough of the arguments, of being without you. I knew I couldn't live without you, whatever you'd done.'

She was amazed. Her pulses skidded dangerously, her heart beating faster. But even if he had thought that, she reasoned, she wouldn't have been able to go back to him, not with that hanging over her head.

Alex walked over to the window and looked out of it broodingly. 'After you walked out of the film, I told myself to forget you, to ignore what I felt.' He looked down at his long hands ruefully. 'But I couldn't. So I got hold of Marney and asked where you'd gone, where you lived. He wouldn't tell me, but when the divorce papers were served on me, I hit the roof!'

I remember, thought Natasha bitterly. The anger had shown in every line of his face when he had come to see her. 'I wondered why you said you wouldn't let me divorce you,' she said truthfully.

He looked away. 'I couldn't stand the thought of losing you,' he said huskily, 'for ever.'

She felt her pulses skip inside her, her head becoming light, but she forced down the feeling of happiness flooding through her and controlled herself.

'After I'd spoken to you about the divorce,' Alex said quietly, 'I thought I'd go out of my mind if I didn't do something pretty quickly to stop you. So I took the first flight back to France and beat the living daylights out of my brother.'

Natasha bit her lip. 'He would have told you of his own accord if you weren't so frightening,' she told him, frowning at the thought of poor Roger being beaten up.

Alex raised dark brows. 'Stop sticking up for him! He deserved a hell of a lot more than he got.' He shrugged. 'I was quite gentle with him, all things considered.'

Natasha frowned. She didn't believe that for a second. She sighed, feeling very confused and anxious. 'Even so,' she said, shaking her head, 'I don't see the point of dropping the divorce case.'

His face hardened. 'Why?' he asked brusquely, thrusting his hands in his pockets and watching her with impenetrable eyes.

She shrugged. 'I couldn't live with you with the threat of mistrust hanging over my head. It could so easily split us up again.'

He came towards her, his face dark and brooding. 'It wouldn't,' he told her firmly, 'I would make damned sure of it.'

Natasha laughed bitterly, raising her eyes to his. 'How, Alex?' she asked. 'What would you do to stop it? Put your hands over your ears so you wouldn't be able to hear it?'

His mouth tightened. 'Don't laugh at me, Natasha,' he said, and his hand reached out to capture her chin, tilting her head up. 'I've put us both through so much pain. I want to make up for it, even though it's difficult.'

She watched him for a moment in silence, then she shook her head. 'No, Alex,' she said huskily, tears forming in the back of her eyes, 'I couldn't risk going through that again.'

His hand tightened on her chin. 'I love you, Natasha,' he said urgently. 'Don't turn me away.'

Her pulse skipped, sending shock waves running through her. But she struggled to control them.

'What else can I do?' she asked huskily. 'How can I go back to a man who doesn't trust me?'

His eyes darkened. 'I'd trust you with my life,'

he muttered. 'I know I've hurt you badly, but you must see that I've been hurt just as much as you. We both went through it together.'

She dropped her gaze. That much was true. She had seen the angry bitterness in his eyes so many times, and seen the pain behind it, knowing it was the root cause of his violence.

She shook her head. 'I don't know, Alex,' she said softly. 'It's too much for me to think about.'

There was a little silence, then Alex took her hand. 'Come with me,' he said darkly, pressing her hand to his mouth, his eyes burning on her. 'I want to show you something.'

She frowned. 'Where?' she asked as he began to lead her out of the house. 'What do you want to show me?'

He opened the front door and they walked out into the sunshine towards his car. 'There's a park round the corner,' he told her as they got into the car. 'I passed it on my way down here.'

Natasha sighed, as they pulled away. She was so confused. She had known all along that Alex still loved her, but the thought of having to go through the last three years again made her wince. It had been too painful. He must understand that.

He pulled up outside the long green metal gates of the park and got out of the car. 'Come on,' he said, taking her hand and leading her out into the street. They went into the park together in silence, and Natasha frowned, wondering why on earth they were here.

'Alex . . .' she began, frowning, but he put a hand to her lips and smiled.

He stopped walking and held her by his side, one long hand curling over her shoulder. 'Do you see that?' he asked gently, pointing up at the sky with one long finger.

Natasha frowned, peering at the glittering orb of the sun framed by a clear blue sky. There was nothing else around, except one or two fluffy white clouds which drifted lazily across the sky, not daring to block out the strength of the sun on a day like this.

'Do you mean the sun?' she asked, raising one eyebrow at him as she turned her head.

Alex smiled. 'Yes,' he said huskily. 'The earth revolves around the sun constantly. Without the sun, the earth would die. It would have no light and no warmth.'

'And?' asked Natasha in a soft voice, her eyes holding his.

Alex's black eyes burned on her. 'You're my sun, Natasha,' he said deeply. 'Without you I'll die. Don't go out of my orbit, because without you I would be nothing.'

Natasha felt her pulses skid, her heart thudding heavily as she listened to his words. She tried to pull herself together, heat flooding through her. 'That's very romantic,' she said shakily, 'but it doesn't solve any of our problems.'

'We'll solve them together,' he urged, his hands caressing her shoulders. 'I can't solve anything without you.'

She avoided his gaze, her face flushing with confusion. 'Stop it, Alex, please,' she begged in a trembling voice.

There was a strained silence. Then his hand captured her chin, tilting her head back to look at him until her long golden hair tumbled back in a shimmering curtain in the sunlight.

His face was tense, his jaw locked tightly. 'Don't leave me, Natasha,' he said in a curiously tense voice. 'I need you. I've loved you from the moment I set eyes on you. I haven't stopped loving you since.'

She caught her breath at the expression in his eyes. 'How . . . how can I think when you look at me like that?' she whispered breathlessly, aware in every bone that she wanted desperately for him to kiss her.

'Easy,' he said thickly. 'You don't think. You just kiss me,' and his mouth closed over hers with a groan, his lips coaxing hers apart beneath him, his hands sliding up and down her back with sensuous, gliding movements. She clung to him hungrily, kissing him back.

After a while he drew his head away, his eyes intent. 'Can you forgive me?' he asked, watching her as though at any moment she would turn him down.

Natasha swallowed. It was either take her chances with both hands and gamble everything she had on him, or walk away and resolve herself to an empty life. Could she ever really forgive him?

He had hated her with a burning intensity only because he had loved her so deeply. His hatred was as strong as his love. And that was what made her mind up for her. When a man loves you as much as that, she reasoned happily, how can you turn him down?

Alex's face was strained, his gaze intent. 'Please,' he said deeply, and a stain of red ran along his hard, controlled cheekbones.

She raised her eyes, feeling a bright scarlet ribbon of happiness wrap around her heart. 'I love you, Alex,' she said simply, smiling up into his eyes.

He closed his eyes tightly on a groan. 'Natasha,' he muttered hoarsely, gathering her into his arms and holding her tight as though afraid she might change her mind, 'I don't deserve this.'

'No, you don't,' she agreed, her cheeks dimpling as she stroked the back of his black head.

Her crushed her against him in silence for a moment, then he whispered against her hair, 'It was all a crazy gamble, coming here. All I had left was hope, because I knew you loved me as much as I loved you. It was just hope that kept me alive trying to find you.' His hands bit into her on a groan of almost physical pain. 'You could so easily have turned me down.'

'But I didn't,' she said, raising her eyes to meet his. His mouth came down to hers, kissing her with an intensity that took her breath away, leaving her reeling, her knees weak.

Later, as they walked back along the path leading out of the park, Natasha looked up at him with a curious frown. 'Why did you bring me here?' she asked, her arm wrapped around his lean waist. 'You could have showed me the sun from Ruth's house.'

Alex grinned and pointed to a sign across the lawn. 'It's called Valentine Park,' he told her sheepishly. 'I thought it might bring me luck.'

She laughed, her eyes twinkling. 'Valentine Park!' she said, her voice teasing him. 'You're an idiot!'

Alex raised his brows, pretending offence. 'Not at all. I thought it was very romantic.'

Natasha's cheeks dimpled, and she turned to stand in front of him, winding her arms around his neck, shivering with delight as his hands slipped sensually around her waist.

'Your trouble,' she told him huskily, 'is that you're a big softy.'

'Am I, indeed?' he muttered thickly. 'We'll soon see about that,' and he bent his head until his mouth touched hers and kissed her until her knees gave way.

ROMANCE

Variety is the spice of romance

Each month, Mills & Boon publish new romances. New stories about people falling in love. A world of variety in romance—from the best writers in the romantic world. Choose from these titles in November.

NORTHERN SUNSET Penny Jordan
A LAMP FOR JONATHAN Essie Summers
SPELLBOUND Margaret Way
LUCIFER'S BRAND Nicola West
THE DEVIL'S MISTRESS Sarah Holland
PASSION FROM THE PAST Carole Mortimer
A TRADITION OF PRIDE Janet Dailey
A MAN OF MEANS Kay Thorpe
MAN FOR HIRE Sally Wentworth
SPRING FEVER Kerry Allyne
ARCTIC ENEMY Linda Harrel
RELUCTANT PARAGON Catherine George

On sale where you buy paperbacks. If you require further information or have any difficulty obtaining them, write to: Mills & Boon Reader Service, PO Box 236, Thornton Road, Croydon, Surrey CR9 3RU, England.

Mills & Boon
the rose of romance

How to join in a whole new world of romance

It's very easy to subscribe to the Mills & Boon Reader Service. As a regular reader, you can enjoy a whole range of special benefits. Bargain offers. Big cash savings. Your own free Reader Service newsletter, packed with knitting patterns, recipes, competitions, and exclusive book offers.

We send you the very latest titles each month, postage and packing free – no hidden extra charges. There's absolutely no commitment – you receive books for only as long as you want.

We'll send you details. Simply send the coupon – or drop us a line for details about the Mills & Boon Reader Service Subscription Scheme. Post to: Mills & Boon Reader Service, P.O. Box 236, Thornton Road, Croydon, Surrey CR9 3RU, England. *Please note: READERS IN SOUTH AFRICA please write to: Mills & Boon Reader Service of Southern Africa, Private Bag X3010, Randburg 2125, S. Africa.

Please send me details of the Mills & Boon Subscription Scheme.

NAME (Mrs/Miss) _____ EP3

ADDRESS _____

_____

COUNTY/COUNTRY_____ POST/ZIP CODE_____

BLOCK LETTERS, PLEASE

Mills & Boon
the rose of romance